The Fatal Eggs

The Fatal Eggs
A Story

Mikhail Bulgakov

Translated by Hugh Aplin

ET REMOTISSIMA PROPE

100 PAGES

100 PAGES
Published by Hesperus Press Limited
4 Rickett Street, London SW6 1RU
www.hesperuspress.com

The Fatal Eggs first published in Russian in 1925 under the title *The Red Ray*
This translation first published by Hesperus Press Limited, 2003

Introduction and English language translation © Hugh Aplin, 2003
Foreword © Doris Lessing, 2003

Designed and typeset by Fraser Muggeridge
Printed in the United Arab Emirates by Oriental Press

ISBN: 1-84391-063-2

CONTENTS

FOREWORD

There were glorious writers in the Stalin period, and some people think Bulgakov was the greatest. *The Master and Margarita* and *The White Guard* are the best known of his works, but this tale, *The Fatal Eggs*, is unfamiliar even to people who love Russian literature and its continuing vitality and inventiveness. Here we have science fiction, pure and simple, but it owes more to the early days of sci-fi and H.G. Wells, whom he admired, than to the spirit shortly to inform the American golden age of science fiction. In the very first line of *The Fatal Eggs* we are told the date of the events is 1928; more precisely, April the 16th. What happening is being commemorated here? 1928 was not the jolliest of years. Much American sci-fi was social criticism or disguised political comment: it has been exasperating to read comments to the effect that science fiction is 'escapist'. It has often fore-shadowed real scientific discovery, and sometimes the horrific regimes it describes have been only too real. *The Fatal Eggs* can be seen as a parable about the nature of Soviet commu-nism, though the frame of the tale is a mad scientist of genius and a ray – not a death ray, but one that vitalises – engendering swarms of reptiles, instead of beneficent beasts, because of some mix-up in the laboratory. This is a device much loved in the genre. At the end, when Moscow is about to be destroyed by the monstrous swarms, it is saved because of a cold snap that destroys the tropical creatures, in the nick of time, just as in *The War of the Worlds* the aliens were opportunely destroyed by a virus they had no defences against, like natives of South America and other innocent places before the coming of the Europeans bearing deadly diseases. No aficionado of the genre could fail to be enchanted by this so perfect example.

When it was written, mad professors of genius and deadly rays were still novelties, embodying the secret fears of ordinary people about what might be going on in the laboratories. This at least hasn't changed, even if nowadays our professors are so urbane and their technologies so confident.

How Bulgakov did enjoy writing *The Fatal Eggs*: the exuberance of it, the enjoyment, has to enliven the reader, and make us laugh! His relish in the tale is like what he brings to *Heart of a Dog*, a more sophisticated story and one which – at least to me – is almost unbearable. Bulgakov was horrified by these amoral scientists. Pavlov was engaged then with his cruel experiments with dogs.

In *The White Guard*, in the midst of the random fighting and arbitrary tides of the civil war, we find ourselves in a laboratory:

'Nikolka took off his cap, noticing the gleaming black blinds drawn down over the windows and a beam of painfully bright light falling on to a desk, behind which was a black beard, a crumpled exhausted face... he glanced nervously around the walls at the line of shiny glass-fronted cabinets containing rows of monstrous things in bottles, brown and yellow, like hideous Chinese faces. Further away stood a tall man, priest-like in a leather apron and black rubber gloves, who was bending over a long table. [...] He stared at the patch of bright light that streamed from the shiny, strangely contorted lamp, and at the other things: at the nicotine-stained fingers and at the repulsive object lying in front of the professor...'

It has to be said that this ugly little scene could be excised from the novel without making any difference to it. Then why is it here? Whatever was the experience or the information that inspired *The Fatal Eggs*, *Heart of a Dog* and this laboratory scene, it went very deep, it must have.

They are protests about the unbearable. Because of the oppression and the censorship of the Soviet regime, nothing could be said openly. *The White Guard,* a realistic novel, had a stormy intermittent life. Fanciful writing had a better chance. *The Master and Margarita* was a protest in imaginative guise. I wonder if that great writer of realistic fiction would have used allegory and disguise at all, had it not been for the censorship? Someone not knowing about the nature of the Soviet regime would have read that book – and these days it is read – without seeing more than 'magic realism' or some such phrase that comforts people who need a tidy shelf with a label to sort out their fiction. But large tracts of it are fact, and it is painful reading, when you know even a little about Soviet reality – know that the book has a basis far from fantasy.

Mikhail Bulgakov was born in Kiev in 1891. He trained for medicine, but instead became a writer – like Anton Chekhov. He began as a journalist, and this served him well with *The White Guard,* whose prose is taut, concise, but lyrical too. *Heart of a Dog*, an early work, was not published in his lifetime in Russian, and not, in fact, until 1987. (He died in 1940.) There could not be a colder, more contemptuous criticism of Soviet reality. A famous but evidently crazy professor adopts a stray dog and gives it a human heart and pituitary gland. But something goes wrong. The dog becomes the cruellest caricature of a boorish and stupid proletarian spouting revolutionary slogans he doesn't understand.

'A man with the heart of a dog,' says a colleague.

'Oh no, no,' says the experimenter, '...for heaven's sake don't insult the dog... [no,] the whole horror of the situation is that now he has a *human* heart, not a dog's heart. And about the rottenest heart in all creation.'

The White Guard was published, then suppressed; the play made from it, *The Days of the Turbins*, was produced in 1926 but then was suppressed. Meanwhile Stalin had seen it fifteen times.

In 1930, worn out with the effort to get his books published and his plays put on, Bulgakov petitioned Stalin to be allowed to emigrate. Stalin telephoned him personally, and arranged a job at the Moscow Arts Theatre. There exists a wonderfully persuasive imagined occasion, describing how Bulgakov was summoned to Stalin's presence in the Kremlin. There sits the renowned but hungry author in his Soviet rags and Stalin is summoning underlings, in the peremptory way of the autocrat, 'How is it our famous writer is in such a state? Somebody's head is going to roll... Bring him food... look at his boots – bring him boots. Bring food... bring champagne...' Bulgakov thinks, 'At last all my troubles are over. He must lift the censorship now.' It is fantasy: funny, painful, true.

A very odd life Stalin did lead with his writers. I have believed for a long time that Stalin wanted to write but had no talent. It would account for his obsession with literature. He personally oversaw everything published in the Soviet Union. He instructed songwriters how to write patriotic songs. Perhaps that famous little black book, such an enigma, really had in it synopses of plots, rhymes for an epic poem, for each stanza would have to end with some rousing thought: destroyed, killing, death sentence, obliterate, confess, assassinate...

Under Stalin, Osip and Nadezhda Mandelshtam, Pasternak, Solzhenitsyn, Akhmatova, Zoshchenko, Babel, and many, many others were murdered, exiled, tortured, tormented, but

Bulgakov was not murdered or tortured or exiled, though he had a bad time of it. If he survived comparatively easily because his portrait of a gentle cultivated family fighting against the Bolsheviks was admired by Stalin, whose efforts to exterminate any vestiges of the intelligentsia were so thorough, then that is the sort of irony that flourishes in mad paradoxical times.

Working at the Moscow Arts Theatre, Bulgakov wrote plays – one about Molière, who had to work, like him, under the eye of the censor – and a novel, *Black Snow*, which was dramatised and performed at the National Theatre in London not long ago: one of the funniest evenings at the theatre I remember. It is about Stanislavsky and his autocratic rule. Bulgakov was no gloomy satirist.

How did Stalin see himself, we may wonder, seeing him like a circus ringmaster with a whip lashing at the constellation of writers Fate or the Logic of History had landed him with? Stalin did tend to go on about writers being the engineers of the human soul, but not one of his poets and word-masters were interested in the kind of Soviet soul he hoped to forge in the fires of Revolution – forgive, but even the mention of Stalin brings on this kind of thing.

The Revolution did badly for Bulgakov in more ways than one. He adored Kiev, evoked so poetically in *The White Guard*, but he did not return to it. Civil war and the necessities of getting a roof over his head and enough to eat kept him in Moscow.

'Mist. Mist, and needle-sharp frost, claw-like frost flowers. Snow, dark and moonless, then faintly paling with the approach of dawn. In the distance beyond the City, blue onion-domes sprinkled with stars of gold leaf; and on its sheer eminence above the City the cross of St Vladimir, only extinguished when the dawn crept in across the Moscow bank of the Dniepr.'

Suppose he had stayed a doctor? There is a little book whose title translates as *Notes of a Young Doctor,* or *A Country Doctor's Notebook,* about a doctor just out of medical school sent to the provinces to a country hospital. He is terrified, knowing his ignorance, but the experienced peasant nurses instruct him in how to do all these things for the first time – deliver a baby, perform dangerous operations. His patients are peasants, uneducated, superstitious, ignorant, 'dark' in mind, and our modern and scientific young doctor is shocked by them. This book has a freshness and liveliness which makes it some people's favourite. An interesting point: the First World War is going on, but its portentous events affect this rural back-water only when a soldier who has run away from the fighting comes home. The little book has an epic quality because of the background of Russia's vastness, the great distances, the weight of the ignorance, the need. You have to read it thinking of the Revolution and the Civil War, just ahead.

War… Civil War… Revolution… Counter Revolution… murders and torture and interrogations, camps and exile and forced labour – infinite suffering, these were the background to Bulgakov's life.

This is how *The White Guard* ends:

'Above the bank of the Dniepr the midnight cross of St Vladimir thrust itself above the sinful, bloodstained, snowbound earth toward the grim, black sky. From far away it looked as if the cross-piece had vanished, had merged with the upright, turning the cross into a sharp and menacing sword.

'But the sword is not fearful. Everything passes away – suffering, pain, blood, hunger and pestilence. The sword will pass away too, but the stars will still remain when the shadows of our presence and our deeds have vanished from the earth. There is no man who does not know that. Why, then, will we not turn our eyes toward the stars? Why?'

– Doris Lessing, 2003

Extracts from *The White Guard* are taken from Mikhail Bulgakov, *The White Guard*, translated by Michael Glenny (Fontana, 1973); extract from *Heart of a Dog* is taken from Mikhail Bulgakov, *The Heart of a Dog*, translated by Michael Glenny (Collins and Harvill Press, 1968).

The Moscow in which Mikhail Bulgakov's story *The Fatal Eggs* unfolds is a place ripe for invasion from the West. Indeed, as the narrative begins in what was, at the time of its writing, the near future of 1928, the incursions of things Western have already begun, ranging from the use of German microscopes to the solution of the housing crisis with American assistance. The very site on which the initial experiments with the so-called 'ray of life' take place is clearly marked as a centre of influence from the West – the Zoological Institute no longer stands on Great Nikitskaya Street, a name redolent of old Moscow, the 'big village' of Russian tradition, for the street has been renamed in honour of Alexander Herzen, the nineteenth-century political thinker who spent much of his adult life abroad, sowing the seeds of revolution with his London-based newspaper *The Bell*.

From the time of Peter the Great onwards, the adoption of Western ideas and ways implied progress and modernity in Russia, and much is made in the story of the modern style of life in Moscow. It is typified by the artificial lights and unnatural sounds that are encountered everywhere, especially in the traffic, whose volume in itself suggests both the increasing speed of twentieth-century existence and the power of technological progress to change the very nature of life. These features are in turn highlighted by the experiments of Professor Vladimir Ipatyevich Persikov that lie at the heart of the story.

Bulgakov specialists have suggested a number of the writer's contemporaries as prototypes for the professor, but it is the identification of Vladimir Ilyich Ulyanov – Lenin – as his inspiration that is most convincing and provocative. The physical description of Persikov is very reminiscent of Lenin; their first name and patronymic (especially when Persikov's patronymic is reduced, as is customary, to Ipatyich) are remarkably similar; their year of birth, 1870, is identical; they both have an obsessive nature. And if Bulgakov's penchant for puckish wordplay and allusion is taken into account, then a link to Lenin can even be found through the professor's seemingly quite unrelated surname, for the scientist entrusted with the task of preserving Lenin's brain after his death in 1924, the year of the composition of *The Fatal Eggs*, was a Professor Abrikosov, his name deriving from the Russian for an apricot, while Persikov derives from the Russian for a peach. And, crucially, Lenin was, of course, in the forefront of the great experiment with Marxist principles in an unsuitable Russian laboratory both before and after his symbolic arrival from the West at the Finland Station in April – the month of Persikov's ill-fated discovery – 1917.

It would be simplistic, however, to regard Persikov merely as the fictionalised incarnation of a fiend who brought Russia to ruin through his importation of Marxist revolution. Apart from anything else, Persikov is closely associated, again in part through names, with various overtly religious notions of divine power, salvation and new life. The Slavonic roots of Vladimir conjure up not only the world domination dreamt of by Lenin and Trotsky, but also the rule of peace (or, indeed, of the peasant commune, a third meaning of the Russian *mir*, which became for Herzen a potential focus for a purely Russian brand of socialism). Ipatyevich comes from the Greek *hypatos*, an epithet regularly associated with Zeus, meaning most high or royal. Persikov lives on Prechistenka, literally 'very pure' (later incongruously renamed Kropotkin Street in honour of the well-known anarchist), on the way to the Smolensk Cathedral of the New Maiden Convent, named in honour of the wonder-working icon of the Virgin of Smolensk. His assistant in the regeneration of the Zoological Institute after the death of the watchman Vlas (from the Greek meaning limp, slow) is the ironically named Pankrat, deriving from the Greek for all-powerful and immediately recalling Pantocrator, the figure of Christ enthroned seen on icons and frescoes. And Persikov's motherly housekeeper is a Russian Mary, while his disciple and ultimate successor in charge of the Institute is a Russian Peter.

Yet nor is Persikov, despite his power over life and the nature of his final fate, a heroic, Christlike figure. It is significant that the huge Church of Christ, situated between Persikov's places of work and residence (and erected to mark the Russian victory over another Western invader, Napoleon Bonaparte), is as irrelevant to him as the sickle moon with which it is regularly associated. For Persikov also represents the Russian intelligentsia, the class whose skills and services were at times courted, at times spurned by a Soviet regime that was suspicious and fearful of its perceived links with bourgeois culture and learning. Thus neither the traditionally Orthodox Russia, nor the Soviet Republic's symbolic sickle can distract Persikov from the focused, but limited vision permitted by the eyepiece of his microscope. And this detachment from the world around him can be seen to be his fatal weakness. Like Pontius Pilate in Bulgakov's most famous work, *The Master and Margarita*, Persikov washes his hands of responsibility at a crucial time, and the dedicated scientist allows his discovery to pass into the hands of Faight, a man who is just as single-minded as Persikov himself, but who lacks the intelligence and the know-how to exploit his determination to beneficial effect.

Faight is the very antithesis of Persikov, the man who knows only one thing, but knows it inside out, for he has performed a whole series of different tasks in the service of the Revolution, but has been moved on from each of them and finally put out to grass by his masters in Moscow. It is his ill-judged and ignorant attempt to adapt Persikov's 'ray of life' for the good of the cause that leads to the perversion of the potentially positive results of the scientist's work. Tellingly, Bulgakov has Faight himself saved by his timely use of the artistic talent he abandoned in favour of revolutionary work – ironically, bourgeois music-making is the one activity for which he has been properly trained. Faight is, incidentally, another character who serves to underline the significance of names in this work, as well as Bulgakov's playful wit. In the Russian text he is Rokk, echoing the Russian word meaning (usually harmful) fate – *rok*. The story's title thus virtually means 'Faight's eggs'. And this in turn could itself be considered a *double entendre*, given the central theme of reproduction, an allusion to Faight's manliness, albeit an ironic one, given his wife's dreamy indifference to him and his chicken-hearted flight from the calamitous situation brought about by his own recklessness. Punning of this sort is also present in, for example, the title of the book's opening chapter, where the first two syllables of the word 'curriculum' echo the Russian word for chickens, a key piece in the zoological jigsaw that leads to the work's chaotic conclusion.

Chaos, confusion and chance – whose power was increasingly recognised by Herzen – are elements which figure throughout *The Fatal Eggs* and stand in contrast to the purported certainties of science, be it zoological or political. It is an accidental combination of circumstances that leads to Persikov's discovery in the first place; the disaster caused by

Faight's annexation of Persikov's equipment is as much the result of a bureaucratic muddle as of Faight's incompetence; and the finale itself shows how easily fate can take an unexpected hand in the course of events. There is some evidence that Bulgakov originally intended to give the story a very different ending, and it may be that its substitution with the existing one, deemed unconvincing by some, was motivated by concerns over censorship; yet its continuation of the theme of unpredictability in affairs on earth surely makes it artistically justified. The confusion and disorientation of life in the modern world are regularly discernible in those scenes on the crowded streets of Moscow, where flashing lights and bestial noises emerge from an environment that is part mechanical, part human, but almost exclusively nameless and faceless. Bulgakov uses the same word, mush, to describe both the mass of creatures produced under the influence of Persikov's ray and the crowds seething in the newly electrified Russian capital. People, even Persikov, are regularly depicted as having voices that sound like animals', and the behaviour of the mob at the end of the story clearly parallels the actions of allegedly lower forms of life. All this is in stark contrast to the tranquil rural life on Faight's State Farm, set up symbolically on the former estate of the aristocratic Sheremetyev family: in this remnant of Russia's pre-revolutionary, pre-twentieth-century past, music spills softly over a subtly moonlit landscape where the driver of the Farm's one vehicle can abandon that intruder from the modern world to make love to an unexpectedly seductive peasant girl.

Although *The Fatal Eggs* evidently represents Bulgakov's reflections on Russia's horrific years of revolution, intervention and civil war, it is nonetheless a work of considerable humour, much of which stems from the satirical barbs directed against early Soviet bureaucracy and the world of journalism that Bulgakov knew so well. And while satire – like another of the author's inspirations here, science fiction – is a genre that can date very rapidly, the topicality of Bulgakov's subject matter for today's reader is quite striking. The sensationalism and economy with the truth demonstrated by sections of the press in the story could scarcely be more familiar; and, of course, the debate on scientific manipulation of the origins of life is of far greater relevance and urgency now than it ever was in the 1920s. And in a world increasingly organised by technology, perhaps the unlikely chance of a major outbreak of fowl plague on the Continent coinciding with the preparation of this translation might even have brought a wry smile to Bulgakov's lips.

– *Hugh Aplin, 2003*

Note on the Text:

The publishing history of this text is a chequered one. It first appeared in the journal *Red Panorama* in 1925 in abridged form, initially under the title *The Red Ray* and subsequently as *The Ray of Life*. That same year it was first published in full in the almanac *The Depths*, and subsequently in Bulgakov's collection of stories *Diaboliad*, only for the collection to be confiscated by the authorities as unsuitable for publication. It was, however, made available in Russia once more in 1926. In 1983 a Russian-language edition was issued in the United States which was based on a photocopy of a typescript apparently authorised by Bulgakov in 1924 and which contained a number of words, phrases and brief passages which the Soviet censors had evidently required to be altered. The original of this typescript has yet to be found, and editions that have since appeared in Russia have included some, all or none of these amendments to the published text of 1926. This translation is based on the fullest possible version of the Russian text.

The Fatal Eggs

CHAPTER ONE
Professor Persikov's Curriculum Vitae

On the evening of the 16th of April 1928, Persikov, Professor of Zoology at the IV State University and Director of the Zoological Institute in Moscow, entered his laboratory, which was located in the Zoological Institute on Herzen Street. The professor switched on the frosted glass ceiling light and looked around him.

The start of the horrifying catastrophe must be considered as having been made specifically on that ill-starred evening, just as the first cause of that catastrophe should be considered to be specifically Vladimir Ipatyevich Persikov.

He was exactly fifty-eight years old. He had a remarkable head, pestle-like, bald, with tufts of yellowish hair sticking out along the sides. He had a clean-shaven face, the lower lip poking forward. Because of this, Persikov's face eternally bore a rather capricious stamp. On a red nose were small old-fashioned glasses in a silver frame, he had brilliant little eyes, was tall, rather stooped. He spoke in a thin, squeaking, croaking voice and had, among other oddities, this one: when he was saying anything weightily and confidently, he turned the index finger of his right hand into a hook and narrowed his little eyes. And as he always spoke confidently, since his erudition in his field was absolutely phenomenal, the hook appeared very frequently before the eyes of Professor Persikov's interlocutors. Whereas outside his field, i.e. zoology, embryology, anatomy, botany and geography, Professor Persikov said almost nothing.

Professor Persikov did not read the newspapers, did not go to the theatre, and the professor's wife had run off with a tenor from Zimin's Opera in 1913, leaving him a note with the following content:

An unbearable shudder of revulsion is aroused in me by your frogs. I shall be unhappy all my life because of them.

The professor did not marry again and had no children. He was very quick-tempered, but relenting, liked tea with cloudberries in it, lived on Prechistenka in a flat with five rooms, one of which was occupied by a wizened little old woman, the housekeeper, Marya Stepanovna, who looked after the professor like a nursemaid.

In 1919 the professor had three of the five rooms taken away from him. He then announced to Marya Stepanovna:

'If they don't stop these outrages, Marya Stepanovna, I shall go abroad.'

There is no doubt that, had the professor realised this plan, he would very easily have been able to secure a place in the Zoology Department of any university in the world, since he was an absolutely first-class scientist, and in the field which one way or another touches upon amphibious or scaleless reptiles even had no equal, with the exception of Professors William Weckle in Cambridge and Giacomo Bartolomeo Beccari in Rome. The professor read four languages besides Russian, and spoke French and German as he did Russian. Persikov did not carry out his intention regarding foreign parts, and the year 1920 turned out even worse than 1919. Events occurred, and, moreover, one after the other. Great Nikitskaya was renamed Herzen Street. Next, the clock cut into the wall of the building on the corner of Herzen Street and Mokhovaya Street stopped at a quarter past eleven, and, finally, in the terrariums of the Zoological Institute, unable to endure all the perturbations of the notable year, there died initially eight magnificent specimens of tree frog, then fifteen common toads, and finally a most exceptional specimen of the Surinam toad.

Immediately after the toads, which wiped out the first order of scaleless reptiles, by rights known as the class of tailless reptiles, there moved on to a better place the Institute's unchanging watchman, old man Vlas, who did *not* belong to the class of scaleless reptiles. The cause of his death, however, was the same as that of the poor reptiles' too, and Persikov identified it immediately:

'Fodderlessness!'

The scientist was absolutely right: Vlas needed to be fed on flour, and the toads on flour worms, but insofar as the former had disappeared, so the latter had vanished as well. Persikov tried to switch the twenty remaining specimens of tree frog to a diet of cockroaches, but the cockroaches, demonstrating their malevolent attitude to war communism, had run off somewhere too. Thus the last specimens also had to be thrown out into the cesspools in the Institute's courtyard.

The effect the deaths, and in particular that of the Surinam toad, had on Persikov beggars description. For some reason he blamed the deaths wholly on the People's Commissar for Enlightenment of the time.[1]

Standing in his hat and galoshes in a corridor of the increasingly cold Institute, Persikov told his assistant, Ivanov, a most elegant gentleman with a fair, pointed little beard:

'You know, killing him for this isn't enough, Pyotr Stepanovich! What on earth are they doing? They'll ruin the Institute, you know! Eh? An incomparable male, an exceptional specimen of *Pipa americana*, thirteen centimetres in length...'

The further things went, the worse they got. After Vlas's death the Institute's windows froze right through, so that floral-patterned ice sat on the inner surface of the panes. The rabbits died, the vixens, the wolves, the fishes and every single grass snake. Persikov started to be silent for days on end, then fell ill with pneumonia, but did not die. When he had recovered, he came to the Institute twice a week and in the circular hall – where it was always, for some reason unchangingly, five degrees below zero, irrespective of what it was outside – wearing galoshes, a hat with ear-flaps and a muffler, exhaling white steam, he gave a course of lectures to an audience of eight on the topic 'Reptiles of the Hot Belt'. All the rest of the time Persikov lay under a travelling-rug on a couch at home on Prechistenka in a room packed to the ceiling with books, coughed and gazed into the mouth of a fiery little stove, which Marya Stepanovna kept stoked with gilded chairs, and thought about the Surinam toad.

But everything under the sun comes to an end. The year 1920 ended, then 1921, and in 1922 a sort of reverse movement began. Firstly, in place of the late Vlas, there appeared Pankrat, a still young, but very promising zoological watchman, and the Institute started little by little to be heated. And in the summer, Persikov, with Pankrat's help, caught fourteen common toads on the River Klyazma. In the terrariums life again came to the boil... In 1923 Persikov was already lecturing eight times a week – three times at the Institute and five at the University, in 1924 thirteen times a week, and in the workers' faculties on top of that, while in 1925, in the spring, he became famous for failing seventy-six students in their exams, and all on scaleless reptiles:

'What do you mean, you don't know how scaleless reptiles

differ from other reptiles?' asked Persikov. 'That is simply ridiculous, young man. Scaleless reptiles have no pelvic gemmae. They are absent. So, sir. Shame on you. You're probably a Marxist?'

'Yes, I am,' replied the victim, fading away.

'So then, if you please, in the autumn,' said Persikov politely, and called brightly to Pankrat: 'Send in the next one!'

In the way that amphibians come to life in the first plentiful rain after a long drought, Professor Persikov came to life in 1926, when a joint Russo-American company built fifteen fifteen-storey buildings in the centre of Moscow, starting at the corner of Gazetny Lane and Tverskaya Street, and three hundred workers' cottages on the outskirts, each with eight apartments, putting an end once and for all to that terrible and ridiculous housing crisis which had been such a torment to Muscovites in the years 1919 to 1925.

In general, that was a remarkable summer in Persikov's life, and at times he rubbed his hands with a quiet and contented tittering, recalling how he and Marya Stepanovna had squeezed into two rooms. Now the professor had been given all five back, he had spread out, set out two and a half thousand books, stuffed animals, diagrams, preparations, and lit the green lamp on the table in the study.

The Institute was unrecognisable too: it had been covered in cream paint, water had been laid on through a special pipe into the reptiles' room, all the glass had been replaced with plate glass, five new microscopes had been sent, glass preparation tables, 2000-watt lamps with indirect light, reflectors, cabinets for the museum.

Persikov came to life, and the whole world unexpectedly learned of this, as soon as, in December 1926, there appeared the pamphlet:

'More on the Question of the Propagation of Gastropods or Chiton', 126 pp. *Proceedings of the IV University.*

And in 1927, in the autumn, came the seminal work of three hundred and fifty pages, translated into six languages, including Japanese:

The Embryology of Pipidae, *Spadefoot Toads and Frogs.* Price 3 roub. State Publishing House.

And in the summer of 1928 there occurred that incredible, dreadful thing…

CHAPTER TWO
The Coloured Helix

And so the professor switched on the light and looked around him. He switched on the reflector on the long experiment table, put on a white coat, clinked some instruments on the table...

Many of the thirty thousand mechanical conveyances running around Moscow in 1928 were rushing by on Herzen Street, rustling over the smooth wooden paving-blocks, and every other minute, with a rumbling and a grinding, a tram of route 16, 22, 48 or 53 would roll down from Herzen Street towards Mokhovaya. It threw reflections of multicoloured lights through the plate glass of the laboratory, and high up and in the distance, alongside the dark and bulky dome of the Church of Christ, could be seen the misty, pale sickle of the moon.

But neither it, nor the rumbling of springtime Moscow interested Professor Persikov in the least. He sat on a revolving three-legged stool and turned with brown tobacco-stained fingers the rack and pinion of a magnificent Zeiss microscope, into which had been placed an ordinary, undyed preparation of fresh amoebae. At the very moment when Persikov was altering the magnification from five to ten thousand, the door opened slightly, a little pointed beard appeared, then a leather apron, and his assistant called:

'Vladimir Ipatyich, I've set up the mesentery, would you like to take a quick look?'

Persikov slid down in lively fashion from the stool, leaving the rack and pinion halfway, and, slowly turning a cigarette in his hands, went through into his assistant's laboratory. There, on the glass table, a frog, half-strangled and stricken with terror and pain, was crucified on a cork base, while its transparent, micaceous entrails had been drawn out of its bloodied stomach into a microscope.

'Very good,' said Persikov, and bent his eye down to the microscope's ocular.

Evidently something very interesting could be made out in the frog's mesentery, where, plain as on the palm of your hand, living blood corpuscles ran busily down the rivers of the blood vessels. Persikov forgot about his amoebae and over the course of an hour and a half, turn by turn with Ivanov, bent down to the microscope's lens. While so doing, the two scientists exchanged words that were animated, but incomprehensible to mere mortals.

Finally Persikov fell back from the microscope, announcing:

'The blood's turning, nothing you can do about it.'

The frog shifted its head ponderously, and its dimming eyes said clearly: 'Bastards, that's what you are...'

Stretching his numb legs, Persikov got up, returned to his laboratory, yawned, rubbed his eternally inflamed eyelids with his fingers, and, having perched on the stool, glanced into the microscope; he laid his fingers on the rack and pinion and was already about to move the screw, but move it he did not. With his right eye Persikov could see a dullish white disc and in it the dim, pale amoebae, but in the middle of the disc sat a coloured helix that resembled a lock of a woman's hair. This helix had been seen by both Persikov himself and hundreds of his students very many times, nobody had been interested in it, and neither was there any reason to have been. The little pencil of coloured light only hindered observation and showed that the preparation was not in focus. Thus with one turn of the screw it was pitilessly erased, and the field was lit with an even, white light. The zoologist's long fingers already lay right against the thread of the screw, but suddenly they jerked and slid off. The reason for this was Persikov's right eye; it had suddenly become wary, astonished, even filled with alarm. Unfortunately for the Republic, it was not third-rate mediocrity that was sitting at the microscope. No, it was Professor Persikov that sat there! The whole of his life and his thoughts were concentrated in his right eye. For some five minutes, in stony silence, a superior being observed an inferior one, tormenting and straining its eye over the preparation that stood out of focus. All around was silent. Pankrat had already fallen asleep in his room in the vestibule, and only once in the distance did the glass of cabinets rattle gently and musically – that was Ivanov locking his laboratory as he left. The street door groaned behind him. Only later was the voice of the professor heard. Whom he asked is unknown.

'What is it? I don't understand a thing...'

A belated lorry passed along Herzen Street, rocking the old walls of the Institute. A shallow glass cup holding tweezers tinkled on the table. The professor turned pale and brought his arms up above the microscope, just as a mother does above a child who is threatened by danger. Now there could be no question at all of Persikov moving the screw, oh no, he was already afraid that some external force might knock what he had seen out of the field of vision.

It was full white morning with a golden strip cutting across the cream porch of the Institute when the professor abandoned his microscope and on numbed legs went up to the window. With trembling fingers he pressed a button, and thick black blinds shut out the morning, and in the laboratory the wise, learned night came to life. A yellow and inspired Persikov spread his legs wide and began to speak, staring at the parquet with watering eyes.

'But how can it be? I mean, it's monstrous!... It's monstrous, gentlemen,' he repeated, addressing the toads in the terrarium, but the toads were asleep and made him no reply.

He was silent for a while, then he went up to the switch, raised the blinds, extinguished all the lights and glanced into the microscope. His face was strained, he knitted his rather bushy yellow eyebrows.

'Aha, aha,' he muttered, 'it's gone. I see. I se-ee,' he drawled out as he gazed, mad and inspired, at the extinguished lamp above his head, 'it's simple.'

And once more he lowered the hissing blinds, and once more switched on the lamp. He glanced into the microscope and gave a joyful and almost predatory grin.

'I'll catch it,' he said solemnly and grandly, raising a finger upwards, 'I will. Perhaps from the sun too.'

Again the blinds went up. The sun was now to hand. It had flooded the walls of the Institute and lain down at an angle on the wooden paving-blocks of Herzen Street. The professor looked out of the window, thinking where the sun would be in the afternoon. Now he would move away, now move closer in a light little dance, and finally he lay his stomach down on the window sill.

He set about important and mysterious work. He covered the microscope with a bell-glass. On the bluish flame of a burner he melted a piece of sealing wax and sealed the edges of the bell-glass to the table, and on the spots of wax he left the imprint of his thumb. He turned off the gas, went out and closed the door of the laboratory on the Yale lock.

There was a half-light in the corridors of the Institute. The professor reached Pankrat's room and knocked at it long and unsuccessfully. Finally, beyond the door could be heard the rumbling of what sounded like a watchdog, hawking and mumbling, and Pankrat, in striped long johns with strings at the ankles, appeared in a bright patch. His eyes stared wildly at the scientist, he was still whimpering slightly from his sleep.

'Pankrat,' said the professor, looking at him over the top of his glasses, 'I'm sorry I woke you up. The thing is, my friend, don't go into my laboratory in the morning. I've left some work there which mustn't be moved. Understood?'

'Oo-ooh, un-un-understood,' replied Pankrat, having understood nothing. He was tottering and growling.

'No, listen, will you wake up, Pankrat,' said the zoologist and poked Pankrat lightly in the ribs, the effect of which was the appearance of fright on his face and a certain shadow of sense in his eyes. 'I've locked the laboratory,' continued Persikov, 'so there's no need to clean it before I arrive. Understood?'

'Yes, sir,' croaked Pankrat.

'Well, that's splendid, now go to bed.'

Pankrat turned, disappeared in the doorway and immediately collapsed onto the bed, while in the vestibule the professor began dressing to go out. He put on a grey summer coat and soft hat, then, remembering the picture in the microscope, he fixed his gaze on his galoshes and looked at them for several seconds, as if he were seeing them for the first time. Then he put the left one on and tried to put the right one onto the left, but it would not fit.

'What a monstrous chance, that he called me away,' said the scientist, 'otherwise I just wouldn't have noticed it. But what does this promise? I mean, it promises the devil knows what!…'

The professor grinned, squinted at his galoshes and took the left one off, while putting the right one on. 'My God! I mean, one can't even imagine all the consequences…' With contempt the professor kicked at the left galosh, which was irritating him by not wanting to fit onto the right one, and set off towards the exit wearing one galosh. At this point he lost his handkerchief and went out, slamming the heavy door. On the porch he spent a long time searching in his pockets for matches by slapping his sides, he found them and moved off along the street with an unlit cigarette in his mouth.

The scientist met not a single person right up until the church. There the professor, tilting his head back, became riveted by the golden helmet-dome. The sun was sweetly licking one side of it.

'How is it I didn't see it before, what chance?... Pah, idiot,' the professor leaned forward and fell into thought, looking at his differently shod feet, 'hm... what shall I do? Go back to Pankrat? No, you won't wake him up. It's a shame to throw the ruddy thing away. I'll have to carry it.' He took the galosh off and started carrying it disdainfully.

Three people drove out from Prechistenka in an old car, two drunks and, on their laps, a woman in loud make-up and the wide silk trousers that were fashionable in 1928.

'Oh dear, daddy-o!' she called in a deep, rather husky voice. 'Why'd you go drinking the proceeds from the other galosh?'

'The old boy's obviously had a skinful in the Alcazar[2],' howled the drunk on the left, and the one on the right poked his head out of the car and shouted:

'Well, dad, is the all-night place on Volkhonka open? That's where we're going!'

The professor looked at them sternly over the top of his glasses, dropped the cigarette from his mouth and immediately forgot about their existence. On Prechistensky Boulevard an aperture of sunshine was being born, and the helmet-dome of Christ began to blaze. The sun had come out.

CHAPTER THREE
Persikov's Caught It

What it was all about was this. When the professor brought his genius' eye close to the ocular, he paid attention for the first time in his life to the fact that one ray in the multicoloured helix stood out particularly brightly and boldly. This ray was bright red in colour and protruded from the helix like a small spike, well, say, the size of a needle, perhaps.

It was just unfortunate that for several seconds this ray riveted the trained eye of the virtuoso.

In it, the ray, the professor made out something that was a thousand times more significant and important than the ray itself, a fragile child, born by chance in the movement of the microscope's mirror and lens. Thanks to the fact that his assistant had called the professor away, the amoebae had lain for an hour and a half under the influence of this ray, and this was what had resulted: whereas on the disc outside the ray the granular amoebae lay around limp and helpless, in the spot where the red sharpened sword fell, strange phenomena were taking place. In the narrow red strip life was on the boil. The little grey amoebae, putting out pseudopodia, pulled themselves with all their might into the red strip and in it (as if by magic) they came to life. Some force breathed the spirit of life into them. They made their way in hordes and fought with one another for a place in the ray. Within it, there was no other word for it, *furious* reproduction was taking place. Breaking and overturning all the laws that Persikov knew like the back of his hand, they gemmated before his eyes at a lightning pace. They split apart in the ray, and each of the parts in the course of two seconds became a new and fresh organism. These organisms achieved growth and maturity in a few moments, only then immediately to produce a new generation in their turn. The red strip, and later the whole disc too, became crowded, and the inevitable struggle began. The newly born went for one another frenziedly, tearing one another to shreds, and swallowing one another. Among those born lay the corpses of those who had perished in the struggle for existence. The best ones and the strong ones were victorious. And these best ones were horrific. Firstly, they were approximately twice the volume of the ordinary amoebae, and secondly, they were distinguished by a particular sort of spite and exuberance. Their movements were speedy, their pseudopodia much longer than the usual ones, and they worked them, without exaggeration, as octopuses do their tentacles.

On the second evening the professor, looking pinched and pale, without food, keeping himself going only with fat roll-ups, studied the new generation of amoebae, while on the third day he moved on to the primary source, that is to the red ray.

The gas hissed quietly in the burner, again the traffic shuffled along the street, and the professor, poisoned by the hundredth cigarette, half closing his eyes, leant onto the back of his revolving armchair.

'Yes, it's all clear now. They were brought to life by the ray. It's a new ray, studied by nobody, discovered by nobody. The first thing that will have to be cleared up is whether it results only from electricity, or from the sun as well,' Persikov muttered to himself.

And in the course of one more night this was cleared up. In three microscopes Persikov caught three rays, caught nothing from the sun and expressed himself thus:

'It must be assumed that it isn't in the spectrum of the sun... hm... well, in short, it must be assumed that it can only be got from electric light.' He looked lovingly at the frosted lamp above; inspired, he had a think and asked Ivanov into his laboratory. He told him everything and showed him the amoebae.

Privat-docent Ivanov was stunned, utterly crushed: how was it that such a simple thing as this slender arrow had not been noticed before, the devil take it! By anyone at all, by him, Ivanov, for example, and it really was monstrous! Just take a look…

'Take a look, Vladimir Ipatyich!' said Ivanov, his eye glued in horror to the ocular. 'What's going on?! They're growing before my eyes… Look, look…'

'This is already the third day I've been observing them…' replied Persikov, inspired.

Then a conversation took place between the two scientists, the sense of which amounted to the following: *Privat-docent* Ivanov undertakes to construct with the aid of lenses and mirrors a chamber in which it will be possible to get this ray in a magnified form and outside the microscope. Ivanov hopes, is even absolutely certain, that this is an extremely simple matter. He will get the ray, Vladimir Ipatyich need have no doubt about it. At this point there was a slight hitch.

'When I publish the work, Pyotr Stepanovich, I shall write that the chamber was constructed by you,' interjected Persikov, sensing that the little hitch needed to be resolved.

'Oh, that's not important… However, of course…'

And the little hitch was immediately resolved. Henceforth the ray absorbed Ivanov too. While Persikov, growing thin and wearing himself out, sat for days and half the nights at the microscope, Ivanov was busy in the physics laboratory, agleam with lamps, testing combinations of lenses and mirrors. He was assisted by a technician.

From Germany, after an enquiry through the Commissariat of Enlightenment, Persikov was sent three parcels containing mirrors, convexo-convex, concavo-concave and even some sort of convexo-concave ground-glass lenses. All this concluded with Ivanov constructing a chamber, and in it he did indeed pick up the red ray. And, to give due credit, picked it up in masterly fashion: the ray came out bold, about four centimetres in diameter, sharp and strong.

On the 1st of June the chamber was set up in Persikov's laboratory, and he greedily began experiments with frog-spawn lit by the ray. These experiments gave amazing results. In the course of two days thousands of tadpoles hatched from the grains of roe. But as if that were not enough, in the course of a single day the tadpoles grew extraordinarily into frogs so vicious and gluttonous that half of them were gobbled up on the spot by the other half. And then those that remained alive began to spawn in no time at all, and in two days, by now without any ray, bred a new generation, and a quite innumerable one at that. In the scientist's laboratory the devil knows what began: tadpoles crawled out from the laboratory and all over the Institute, in the terrariums and simply on the floor, in every cranny, shrill choirs set up a howling, as in a swamp. Pankrat, who feared Persikov like fire as it was, now experienced in relation to him a single feeling: mortal dread. After a week even the scientist himself felt that he was going crazy. The Institute was filled with the smell of ether and potassium cyanide, which almost poisoned Pankrat when he took off his mask at the wrong time. It finally proved possible to slaughter the spreading swamp generation with poisons and to air the laboratories.

Persikov spoke thus to Ivanov:

'You know, Pyotr Stepanovich, the effect of the ray on

deutoplasm and in general on the ovule is astonishing.'

Ivanov, a cold and restrained gentleman, interrupted the professor in an unusual tone:

'Vladimir Ipatyich, why is it you're talking about minor details, about deutoplasm? Let's speak frankly: you've discovered something unheard of,' and it was clearly a great effort, but still Ivanov forced the words out of himself: 'Professor Persikov, you've discovered the ray of life!'

A faint colour appeared on Persikov's pale, unshaven cheek-bones.

'Now, now, now,' he muttered.

'You'll…' continued Ivanov, 'you'll make yourself such a name… My head's spinning. You see,' he continued passion-ately, 'Vladimir Ipatyich, Wells's heroes in comparison with you are simply nonsense… And there was I thinking that it was fairy tales… You remember his *The Food of the Gods*[3]?'

'Ah, that's a novel,' replied Persikov.

'Well yes, good Lord, it's famous!…'

'I've forgotten it,' replied Persikov, 'I remember I've read it, but I've forgotten it.'

'How can you fail to remember, just take a look,' and from the glass table Ivanov picked up by the leg a dead frog of unbelievable size with a swollen belly. Even in death there was a malicious expression on its face. 'This is just monstrous, you know!'

CHAPTER FOUR

Thrushova the Priest's Widow

God knows why, whether Ivanov was to blame here, or because sensational news items are transmitted through the air of their own accord, but, in the gigantic, seething city of Moscow, people suddenly began talking about the ray and about Professor Persikov. Somehow in passing and very hazily, it is true. News of the miraculous discovery jumped like a bird with a gunshot wound in the gleaming city, now disappearing, now soaring up once more, until the middle of July, when on page twenty of the newspaper *Izvestiya*, under the heading 'Scientific and Technical News', there appeared a brief notice dealing with the ray. It was stated blankly that a well-known professor at the IV University had invented a ray which produced an incredible increase in the vital activity of inferior organisms, and that this ray required testing. The surname was garbled, of course, and they printed 'Pevsikov'.

Ivanov brought in the newspaper and showed Persikov the notice.

' "Pevsikov",' grumbled Persikov, busy with the chamber in his laboratory, 'how is it these layabouts know everything?'

Alas, the garbled surname did not save the professor from events, and they began on the very next day, immediately violating the whole of Persikov's life.

Pankrat, after giving a preliminary knock, appeared in the laboratory and handed Persikov the most magnificent satin visiting-card.

''e's out there,' added Pankrat timidly.

On the card in an elegant font was printed:

Alfred Arkadyevich
Bronsky
Contributor to the Moscow journals
The Red Light, The Red Pepper, The Red Journal,
The Red Searchlight
and the newspaper
The Red Evening Newspaper.

'Send him to the devil,' said Persikov in a monotone, and flicked the card under the table.

Pankrat turned, went out, and five minutes later returned with a long-suffering face and with a second copy of the same card.

'Are you trying to be funny?' shrilled Persikov, turning ugly.

'From the esspeedee, 'e says,' replied Pankrat, growing pale.

Persikov seized the card with one hand and almost tore it in half, while with the other he flung his tweezers onto the table. On the card in an ornate script was added: 'I very much ask and excuse myself to be seen, esteemed Professor, for three minutes on a public matter of the press and contributor to the satirical journal *Red Raven*, publication of the SPD[4].'

'Call him in here,' said Persikov and gasped for breath.

Immediately there popped out from behind Pankrat's back a young man with a clean-shaven, oily face. One was struck by the eyebrows, eternally raised like a Chinaman's, and beneath them the agate-coloured little eyes that did not look the person he was talking to in the eye for even a second. The young man was dressed quite irreproachably and fashionably in a narrow, knee-length jacket, extremely wide bell-bottom trousers and lacquered boots of unnatural width with toes resembling hooves. In his hands the young man held a walking-stick, a hat with a sharp point and a notebook.

'What do you want?' asked Persikov, in such a voice that Pankrat instantly went out of the door. 'You were told that I'm busy, weren't you?'

Instead of replying, the young man bowed to the professor twice, to the left-hand side and to the right, and then his little eyes skimmed around the whole laboratory like a wheel, and immediately the young man made a mark in his notebook.

'I'm busy,' said the professor, looking into his guest's little eyes with revulsion, but he achieved no effect, since the little eyes were elusive.

'A thousand pardons, most esteemed professor,' began the young man in a thin voice, 'for my bursting in on you and taking up your precious time, but the news of your world-class discovery, that has resounded throughout the entire world, forces our journal to ask you for some explanations.'

'What explanations are these throughout the entire world?' whined Persikov shrilly, and turning yellow. 'I'm not obliged to give you explanations or anything of the kind... I'm busy... terribly busy.'

'And what is it you're working on then?' asked the young man sweetly, and made a second mark in the notebook.

'I... what is it? Do you want to print something?'

'Yes,' replied the young man, and suddenly began scribbling in the notebook.

'Firstly, I don't intend publishing anything until I finish my work... least of all in these newspapers of yours... Secondly, how do you know all this?...' And Persikov suddenly felt he was becoming flustered.

'Is the news that you've discovered the ray of new life accurate?'

'What new life is that?' cried the professor in a frenzy. 'Why are you talking rot? The ray on which I'm working is still far from fully researched, and in general nothing is known as yet! It's possible that it increases the vital activity of protoplasm…'

'By how many times?' asked the young man hurriedly.

Persikov became completely flustered… 'What a fellow! I mean, this is the devil knows what!' he thought.

'What are these ignorant questions?… Let's suppose I say, well, a thousand times!…'

In the young man's little eyes there was a flash of predatory joy.

'Do gigantic organisms result?'

'Nothing of the sort! Well, it's true, the organisms I've got are bigger than normal… Well, they have certain new characteristics… But after all, the main thing here isn't the size, but the incredible speed of reproduction,' said Persikov to his cost, and was at once horrified. The young man covered a whole page in writing, turned it over and began scribbling away some more.

'Now, will you stop writing!' croaked Persikov in despair, already submitting and feeling that he was in the young man's hands. 'What is it you're writing?'

'Is it true that in the course of two days it's possible to get two million tadpoles from spawn?'

'From what quantity of spawn?' shouted Persikov, becoming enraged once more. 'Have you ever seen a grain of roe… well, shall we say of a frog?'

'From half a pound?' asked the young man, unabashed.

Persikov turned crimson.

'And who measures like that? Pah! What are you saying? Well, of course, if you took half a pound of frog-spawn… then maybe… damnation, well, about that quantity, or perhaps even a lot more!'

Diamonds lit up in the young man's eyes, and in a single flourish he covered yet another page with scribbles.

'Is it true that this will cause a world revolution in animal husbandry?'

'What sort of journalistic question is that?' howled Persikov, 'and in general I'm not giving you permission to write rot. I can see by your face that you're writing something abominable!'

'I most earnestly request your photograph, Professor,' pronounced the young man, and slammed his notebook shut.

'What? My photograph? That's for your paltry journals? Together with this damned idiocy you're writing there? No, no, no... And I'm busy... I must ask you!...'

'An old one at least. And we'll return it to you instantly.'

'Pankrat!' shouted the professor in fury.

'I have the honour to take my leave,' said the young man, and vanished.

Instead of Pankrat, from beyond the door came the strange, regular creaking of a machine, a terse knocking on the floor, and there appeared in the laboratory a man of unusual corpulence, dressed in a smock and trousers made out of blanket cloth. His left, mechanical leg clicked and rumbled, while in his hands he held a briefcase. His round, shaved face, filled with yellowish flab, presented a friendly smile. He bowed to the professor and straightened up in military fashion, as a result of which his leg emitted a springy click. Persikov was dumbstruck.

'Mr Professor,' began the stranger in a pleasant, slightly husky voice, 'forgive the mere mortal who has infringed upon your solitude.'

'Are you a reporter?' asked Persikov. 'Pankrat!!'

24

'Not at all, Mr Professor,' replied the fat man, 'allow me to introduce myself – captain of ocean-going ships and contributor to the Council of People's Commissars' newspaper, *The Herald of Industry*.'

'Pankrat!!' shouted Persikov hysterically, and straight away in the corner the telephone threw out its red signal and gave a soft ring. 'Pankrat!' repeated the professor. 'Hello.'

'*Verzeihen Sie, bitte, Herr Professor*,' croaked the telephone in German, '*dass ich störe. Ich bin Mitarbeiter des Berliner Tagesblatts…*[5]'

'Pankrat!' shouted the professor into the receiver, '*Bin momentan sehr beschäftigt und kann Sie deshalb jetzt nicht empfangen!…*[6] Pankrat!!'

And at this point the ringing started at the main entrance to the Institute.

* * *

'Nightmare murder on Bronnaya Street!!' howled unnatural hoarse voices, moving in the dense mass of lights among the wheels and flashes of lamps on the heated June roadway, 'nightmare outbreak of chicken disease at priest's widow Thrushova's with her picture!… Nightmare discovery of Professor Persikov's ray of life!!'

Persikov made such a dash that he almost went under a car on Mokhovaya, and seized a newspaper in a frenzy.

'Three kopeks, citizen!' shouted the little boy and, squeezing his way into the crowd on the pavement, began to howl once more: '*Red Evening Newspaper*, discovery of X-ray!!'

A stunned Persikov opened out the newspaper and pressed up against a lamppost. In a smudged frame in the left-hand corner on page two a man glanced at him, bald, with mad and unseeing eyes and a drooping lower jaw, the fruit of the artistic creativity of Alfred Bronsky. 'V.I. Persikov, discoverer of the mysterious red ray' read the caption under the drawing. Lower down, under the heading 'Mystery on a World Scale', the article began with the words:

' "Do sit down," the eminent scientist Persikov said to us in friendly fashion...'

The article sported at its foot the signature: 'Alfred Bronsky (Alonso)'.

A greenish light flew up above the roof of the university, the fiery words '*The Talking Newspaper*' leapt out in the sky, and a crowd immediately filled Mokhovaya to overflowing.

'Do sit down!!!' suddenly howled in a loudspeaker on the roof a most unpleasant thin voice, just like the voice of Alfred Bronsky, magnified a thousand times, 'the eminent scientist Persikov said to us in friendly fashion! I have long wanted to acquaint the Moscow proletariat with the results of my discovery...'

A quiet mechanical creaking was heard behind Persikov's back, and somebody pulled at his sleeve. Turning, he saw the yellow, round face of the owner of the mechanical leg. The latter's eyes were moistened with tears, and his lips were quivering.

'You did not wish to acquaint *me*, Mr Professor, with the results of your amazing discovery,' he said sadly, and sighed deeply. 'I've lost my fifteen roubles.'

He gazed mournfully at the roof of the university, where the invisible Alfred was ranting in the black jaws. For some reason Persikov began to feel sorry for the fat man.

'I,' he muttered, catching the words from the sky with hatred, 'didn't say any "sit down" to him! He's simply an insolent wretch of an extraordinary nature! You'll forgive me, please, but really, when you're working, and people burst in… I'm not talking about you, of course…'

'Perhaps, Mr Professor, you'll at least give me a description of your chamber?' said the mechanical man ingratiatingly and dolefully. 'After all, it makes no difference to you now…'

'From half a pound of spawn such a quantity of tadpoles hatches out in the course of three days that there is absolutely no chance of counting them,' roared the invisible being in the loudspeaker.

'Toot, toot,' called the cars on Mokhovaya indistinctly.

'Ho, ho, ho… How about that, ho, ho, ho,' rustled the crowd, tilting back their heads.

'What sort of a swine is that? Eh?' hissed Persikov, trembling with indignation, to the mechanical man. 'How do you like that? Well, I shall be making a complaint about him!'

'Disgraceful!' concurred the fat man.

The most blinding violet ray struck the professor's eyes, and everything around flared up – the lamppost, a section of the woodblock roadway, a yellow wall, curious faces.

'It's you, Mr Professor,' whispered the fat man admiringly, and hung on the professor's sleeve like a lead weight. In the air something began to rattle.

'Ah, they can all go to the devil!' exclaimed Persikov mournfully, extricating himself from the crowd together with the lead weight. 'Hey, taxi-cab. To Prechistenka!'

The peeling old car of 1924 construction began gurgling by the pavement, and the professor climbed into the back, attempting to detach himself from the fat man.

'You're hindering me,' he hissed, and took cover from the violet light behind his fists.

'Read it?! What they're yellin' about?… Professor Persikov and 'is kids've 'ad their throats cut on Little Bronnaya!…' people were shouting in the crowd all around.

'I don't have any kids, the sons of bitches,' yelled Persikov, and suddenly came into the focus of a black camera, which shot him in profile with open mouth and frenzied eyes.

'Crk… toot… crk… toot,' the taxi-cab called out, and cut into the dense mass.

The fat man was already sitting in the back of the cab and warming the professor's side.

CHAPTER FIVE
The Chicken Business

In the insignificant little provincial town formerly called Trinitysk, now Opticovsk, in the Opticovsk District of Kostroma Province, onto the little porch of a little house on the former Cathedral, now Karl Radek[7] Street, there emerged a woman with her hair tied in a headscarf, wearing a grey cotton dress printed with bunches of flowers, who burst into sobs. This woman, the widow of Thrushov, the former cathedral archpriest of the former cathedral, sobbed so loudly that soon a peasant woman's head in a downy shawl poked out of a window in the little house across the street and exclaimed:

'What's up, Stepanovna, not another one?'

'The seventeenth!' replied the former Thrushova, over-flowing with sobs.

'Lackaday-ka-day-ka,' the peasant woman in the scarf began wailing and shaking her head, 'what on earth can it be then? The Lord's angry, that's the truth of it! But surely it can't be dead?'

'You just take a look, take a look, Matryona,' mumbled the priest's widow, blubbering loudly and deeply, 'you take a look at what's up with it.'

A crooked grey gate slammed, the peasant woman's bare feet slapped over the dusty humps of the street, and the priest's widow, wet with tears, led Matryona into her poultry yard.

It must be said that the widow of the archpriest Father Savvaty Thrushov, who died in 1926 of antireligious propaganda, had not lost heart, but had founded the most remarkable poultry-breeding business. No sooner had the widow's affairs taken an upward turn than the widow was burdened with such a tax that the poultry-breeding very nearly ceased, but for some good people. They gave the widow the idea of submitting a statement to the local authorities to the effect that she, the widow, was founding a workers' poultry-breeding *artel*. The personnel of the *artel* comprised Thrushova herself, her faithful servant Matryoshka and the widow's deaf niece. The tax was withdrawn from the widow, and the poultry-breeding flourished to such an extent that by 1928 in the widow's dusty little yard, fringed with little hen-houses, there were as many as two hundred and fifty hens, among which there were even some cochin-chinas. The widow's eggs appeared each Sunday at the Opticovsk market, the widow's eggs were traded in Tambov, and they sometimes even made an appearance in the glass shop windows of the former 'Chichkin's Cheese and Butter in Moscow'.

And now the seventeenth brahma since the morning, her favourite tufted one, was walking around the yard vomiting. 'Er... rr... oorl... oorl ho-ho-ho,' was what Tufty was doing, and it was screwing its sad eyes up at the sun, as if seeing it for the last time. On her haunches in front of the hen's nose danced *artel* member Matryoshka with a cup of water.

'Dear little Tufty... cluck, cluck, cluck... have a nice little drop of water,' begged Matryoshka, and chased after Tufty's beak with the cup, but Tufty did not wish to drink. It was opening its beak wide, craning its head up. Then it began vomiting blood.

'Oh Lord Jesus!' exclaimed the guest, slapping her hips. 'What on earth is going on? Just spouting blood. I've never seen – strike me down if I have – a hen suffering with its stomach like a person.'

And these were the last words to send poor Tufty on its way. It suddenly tumbled over onto its side, pecked helplessly at the dust with its beak and rolled its eyes. Then it turned over onto its back, stuck both legs up in the air and remained motionless. Matryoshka, slopping water from the cup, burst out crying in her bass voice, as did the priest's widow herself, the *artel* president, but the guest bent down to her ear and began whispering:

'Stepanovna, I'll eat my hat if your hens haven't been given the evil eye. Where have you seen such a thing? I mean, there aren't any such chicken diseases! It's someone's put a spell on your hens.'

'My mortal enemies!' exclaimed the priest's widow to the heavens. 'What, do they want to be the death of me?'

Her words were answered by the loud cry of a cockerel, and then there tore out from a hen-coop – sideways somehow, like a disorderly drunk from a beer bar – a tatty, wiry cockerel. It stared at them wildly, clawed at the ground, spread its wings wide, like an eagle, yet did not fly off anywhere, but began running around the yard, in a circle, like a horse on a lunge. On the third circuit it stopped and was sick, then it began hawking and wheezing, spat out spots of blood all around itself, turned on its back, and pointed its legs up at the sun like masts. Women's howling filled the yard. And it was answered in the little hen-houses by an uneasy clucking, flapping and fidgeting.

'Well, isn't that the evil eye?' asked the guest triumphantly. 'Call in Father Sergiy, let him conduct a service.'

At six o'clock in the evening in the poultry-breeding yard, when the sun sat low like a fiery face among the faces of the young sunflowers, Father Sergiy, the senior priest of the cathedral church, having finished his service, was struggling out of his stole. People's curious heads poked up above, and through gaps in the ancient fence. The grieving priest's widow, with her lips pressed against a cross, abundantly moistened a torn, canary-yellow rouble with her tears and handed it to Father Sergiy, at which he, sighing, made some remark to the effect that 'well, God is angry with us'. In so doing, Father Sergiy looked as if he knew perfectly well why the Lord was angry, only would not tell.

After this the crowd dispersed from the street, and since chickens go to bed early, nobody even knew that in the hen-coop of priest's widow Thrushova's neighbour three hens and a cockerel had died all at once. They had vomited just like Thrushova's hens, only their deaths had occurred in a closed hen-coop and quietly. The cockerel had toppled headfirst from his perch and expired in that position. As regards the widow's hens, they were finished off immediately after the service, and by the evening all was dead and quiet in the hen-coops, the stiffened poultry lay in heaps.

In the morning the town rose as if thunderstruck, because the business assumed strange and monstrous proportions. By noon only three chickens remained alive on Karl Radek Street, in the end house, where the district inspector of finance rented an apartment, but those too had died by one o'clock in the afternoon. And by the evening the little town of Opticovsk was humming and seething like a hive, and through it flew the dread word 'pestilence'. Thrushova's name got into the local newspaper *The Red Fighter* in an article under the headline 'Could it be Fowl Plague?', and from there it all sped on to Moscow.

* * *

Professor Persikov's life assumed a strange, disturbed and worrying complexion. In short, it was simply impossible to work in such a situation. The day after he had finished with Alfred Bronsky, he was obliged to disconnect the telephone in his laboratory at the Institute by taking it off the hook, and in the evening, while travelling in a tram along Okhotny Row, the professor caught sight of himself on the roof of a huge building with the black inscription '*The Workers' Newspaper*'. He, the professor, breaking up and turning green and blinking, was climbing into the back of a taxi, and after him, clutching at his sleeve, climbed a mechanical ball in a blanket. The professor on the roof, on a white screen, was shielding himself with his fists from a violet ray. After this there leapt out a fiery inscription: 'Professor Persikov, riding in an auto, gives an explanation to our renowned reporter, Captain Stepanov.' And indeed: past the Church of Christ, along Volkhonka Street, sped a shaky automobile, and in it floundered the professor, and his physiognomy was like that of a wolf at bay.

'They're devils of some sort, not people,' muttered the zoologist through his teeth, and rode past.

That same day, in the evening, on returning to his home on Prechistenka, the zoologist received from his housekeeper, Marya Stepanovna, seventeen notes with the telephone numbers that had rung him during his absence, and the verbal declaration of Marya Stepanovna that she was worn out. The professor wanted to tear the notes to pieces, but paused, because against one of the numbers he caught sight of the additional note: 'People's Commissar for Health'.

'What is all this?' thought the eccentric scientist in genuine puzzlement. 'What's happened to them?'

At a quarter past ten that same evening the bell rang, and the professor was forced to converse with a certain citizen, dazzling in his attire. The professor received him thanks to his visiting-card, on which there figured (without first name or surname): 'Plenipotentiary Head of Trade Departments of Foreign Representative Bodies in the Soviet Republic'.

'I wish the devil would take him,' growled Persikov, threw his magnifying glass and some diagrams onto the green cloth, and said to Marya Stepanovna: 'Call him in here, into the study, this plenipotentiary person.'

'How can I help?' asked Persikov in such a voice that the Head was somewhat convulsed. Persikov transplanted his spectacles from the bridge of his nose to his forehead, then back again, and examined the visitor. The latter shone all over with lacquer and precious stones, and in his right eye there sat a monocle. 'What a vile mug,' thought Persikov for some reason.

The guest began in a roundabout way, namely by asking permission to smoke a cigar, in consequence of which Persikov with great unwillingness invited him to sit down. Next the guest pronounced a long apology regarding the fact that he had come so late: 'but it is quite impossible for Mr Professor to be caugh... hee-hee... pardon me... found during the day' (the guest, when laughing, sobbed like a hyena).

'Yes, I'm busy!' replied Persikov so curtly that for a second time a spasm ran through the guest.

Nonetheless, he permitted himself to disturb the renowned scientist.

'Time is money, as they say... The cigar doesn't bother the professor?'

'Murr-murr-murr,' replied Persikov. He had given permission...

'The professor has discovered the ray of life, hasn't he?'

'Forgive me, what life is that?! That's the invention of journalists!' Persikov became animated.

'Oh no, hee-hee-hee…' he understands perfectly the modesty that comprises the true adornment of all genuine scientists… there can be no argument… There are telegrams today… In the cities of the world, namely Warsaw and Riga, everything is already known regarding the ray. The name of Prof. Persikov is being repeated by the whole world… The whole world is following Prof. Persikov's work with bated breath… But it is perfectly well known to everyone how hard the position of scientists is in Soviet Russia. *Entre nous soit dit*[8]… There are no outsiders here?… Alas, they don't know how to value scientific labours here, and so he would like to have a discussion with the professor… A certain foreign state is offering Professor Persikov entirely disinterested assistance in his laboratory work. Why cast your pearls here, as the Holy Scriptures say? The state knows how hard things were for the professor in 1919 and 1920 during this, hee-hee… revolution. Well, of course, a strict secret… the professor will acquaint the state with the results of his work, and in return for this it finances the professor. He has built a chamber, has he not, so it would be interesting to familiarise oneself with the plans of this chamber…

And here the guest pulled from an inside pocket of his jacket a snowy-white bundle of notes…

Some trifle, five thousand roubles, for example, as an advance, the professor can receive this very minute… and no receipt required… the professor will even offend the Plenipotentiary Trade Chief if he mentions a receipt.

'Out!!!' Persikov suddenly barked so fearsomely that the high keys of the piano in the drawing-room emitted a sound.

The guest vanished in such a way that, a minute later, Persikov, trembling with rage, was already himself in doubt as to whether he had been there or had been a hallucination.

'His galoshes?!' howled Persikov a minute later in the entrance hall.

'He forgot them,' replied the trembling Marya Stepanovna.

'Throw them out!'

'How am I to throw them out? He'll come to get them.'

'Hand them in to the house committee. Get a receipt. I want no trace of these galoshes! To the committee! Let them take the spy's galoshes!…'

Marya Stepanovna, crossing herself, gathered up the magnificent leather galoshes and carried them away to the rear entrance. There she stood for a little while outside the door, and then hid the galoshes in the larder.

'Handed them in?' stormed Persikov.

'Yes.'

'Give me the receipt.'

'But, Vladimir Ipatyich. But the President is illiterate!…'

'Get-a–receipt–this–instant. Let some literate son of a bitch sign it on his behalf!'

Marya Stepanovna only turned her head a little, went away and returned after fifteen minutes with a note:

'Received into stock from Prof. Persikov 1 (one) pa galo. Kolesov.'

'And what's this?'

'A token, sir.'

Persikov trampled on the token, but put the receipt away under a paper-press. Then some thought clouded his steeply sloping forehead. He rushed to the telephone, rang up Pankrat at the Institute and asked him: 'Is all well?' Pankrat growled something into the receiver, from which it could be understood that, in his opinion, all was well. But Persikov was reassured only for a minute. Frowning, he grabbed the telephone and said the following into the receiver:

'Give me the, what's it called, the Lubyanka[9]. *Merci*... Which of you there do I need to tell... I've got some suspicious types in galoshes coming here, and... Professor Persikov of the IV University –'

The receiver suddenly broke off the conversation abruptly. Persikov stepped back, mumbling some curses through his teeth.

'Will you be having some tea, Vladimir Ipatyich?' enquired Marya Stepanovna timidly, glancing into the study.

'No, I will not be having any tea... murr-murr-murr, and the devil take the lot of them... how mad they were, though.'

Exactly ten minutes later the professor was receiving new guests in his study. One of them, pleasant, round and very polite, was wearing a modest khaki military service jacket and breeches. On his nose, like a crystal butterfly, sat a pince-nez. In general, he was reminiscent of an angel in lacquered boots. The second, quite short and terribly gloomy, was in plain clothes, but the plain clothes sat on him as if they constrained him. The third guest behaved peculiarly, he did not enter the professor's study, but remained in the semi-darkness of the entrance hall. At the same time the study, illuminated and permeated with streams of tobacco smoke, was visible to him throughout. The face of this third, who was also in plain clothes, sported a smoked-glass pince-nez.

The two in the study wore Persikov out completely, examining the visiting-card, asking questions about the five thousand and making him describe the guest's appearance.

'The devil knows,' grumbled Persikov, 'just a disagreeable physiognomy. A degenerate.'

'And did he have a glass eye?' asked the small one hoarsely.

'The devil knows. But no, not glass, shifty eyes.'

'Rubinstein?' the angel addressed the little plain-clothes

man quietly and enquiringly. But the latter shook his head gloomily and negatively.

'Rubinstein wouldn't give it without a receipt, not in any circumstances,' he mumbled, 'this isn't Rubinstein's work. There's someone rather bigger here.'

The story of the galoshes elicited an explosion of the most lively interest on the part of the guests. The angel uttered just a few words into the telephone of the house-manager's office: 'The State Political Directorate summons the secretary of the house-management committee Kolesov to Professor Persikov's apartment this minute with the galoshes' – and Kolesov, pale, immediately appeared in the study, holding the galoshes in his hands.

'Vasenka!' the angel called in a low voice to the one sitting in the entrance hall. The latter got up sluggishly and, seemingly unsteady, trudged into the study. The smoked glass completely absorbed his eyes.

'Well?' he asked laconically and sleepily.

'The galoshes.'

The smoky eyes slid over the galoshes, and, as they did, it seemed to Persikov that from under the glasses there was a momentary sidelong flash of by no means sleepy, but, on the contrary, astonishingly sharp eyes. But they went out instantly.

'Well, Vasenka?'

The one they called Vasenka answered in a sluggish voice:

'Well, why the well? Pelenzkowski's galoshes.'

The house committee's stock was immediately deprived of Professor Persikov's present. The galoshes disappeared in newspaper. The extremely gladdened angel in the service jacket rose and began shaking the professor's hand, and even made a little speech, the content of which amounted to the following: this does the professor honour... the professor can rest assured... nobody will trouble him any more, neither at the Institute, nor at home... measures will be taken, his chambers are in the most complete safety.

'And is it not possible for you to shoot the reporters?' asked Persikov, looking over the top of his glasses.

This question amused the guests greatly. Not only the gloomy small one, but even the tinted one in the entrance hall smiled. The angel, sparkling and beaming, explained that for the moment, hm... of course, it would be a good thing... but, you see, the press, after all... although, actually, a plan like that is already taking shape in the Council of Labour and Defence... we have the honour to take our leave.

'And who was the scoundrel that came to see me?'

At this point everybody stopped smiling, and the angel replied evasively that it was just some petty conman, that it was not worth paying any attention... nonetheless he earnestly begged the citizen professor to keep this evening's occurrence an absolute secret, and the guests left.

Persikov returned to his study and the diagrams, but still he was not to get down to work. The telephone threw out a fiery little ring, and a woman's voice offered the professor – should he wish to marry a good-looking and passionate widow – a seven-room apartment. Persikov howled into the receiver:

'I advise you to get treatment from Professor Rosso-limo[10]...' – and received another call.

Here Persikov softened somewhat, because it was quite a well-known figure ringing from the Kremlin, who questioned Persikov long and sympathetically about his work and expressed a desire to visit the laboratory. Leaving the telephone, Persikov wiped his forehead and took the receiver off the hook. Then, in the apartment above, strange trumpets began to rumble and the shrieks of Valkyries began to fly – the radio receiver of the director of a textile trust had picked up the Wagner concert in the Bolshoi Theatre. To the howling and crashing that poured down from the ceiling, Persikov announced to Marya Stepanovna that he would take the director to court, would break that receiver for him, would leave Moscow and go to the devil, because people had evidently made up their minds to drive him away. He smashed his magnifying glass, lay down to sleep on the couch in the study and fell asleep to a renowned pianist's gentle tinkling of the keys, flying in from the Bolshoi Theatre.

The surprises continued on the following day too. Arriving by tram at the Institute, Persikov found on the porch a citizen unfamiliar to him, wearing a fashionable green bowler hat. The latter scrutinised Persikov attentively, but did not address any questions to him, and for that reason Persikov suffered him. But in the entrance hall of the Institute, besides the bewildered Pankrat, a second bowler hat rose to meet Persikov and greeted him politely:

'Hello, Citizen Professor.'

'What do you want?' asked Persikov fearsomely, stripping off his coat with Pankrat's assistance. But the bowler hat quickly pacified Persikov, whispering in the gentlest of voices that the professor had no reason to worry. He, the bowler hat, was there specifically to save the professor from importunate visitors of any sort… that the professor could rest assured, not only in respect of the laboratory doors, but also in respect of the windows. After this the unknown man turned back the breast of his jacket for a moment and showed the professor some sort of badge.

'Hm… yes, you've got things really well organised,' bellowed Persikov, and added naively: 'And what will you have to eat here?'

At this the bowler hat grinned and explained that somebody would relieve him.

The next three days went magnificently. The professor had visitors from the Kremlin twice, and once there were students whom Persikov examined. The students were failed to the very last one, and it was clear from their faces that Persikov now aroused in them a simply superstitious dread.

'Go and be a bus conductor! You're incapable of studying zoology,' carried from the laboratory.

'Strict?' the bowler hat asked Pankrat.

'Lor' lumme,' replied Pankrat, 'if anybody *does* pass, the fellow comes staggerin' out of the lab. He's sweatin' like a pig. And he's straight down the beer bar.'

With all these little bits of business the professor did not notice the three days, but on the fourth he was returned to real life once more, and the cause of this was a thin and shrill voice from the street.

'Vladimir Ipatyich!' cried the voice from Herzen Street through the open window of the laboratory. The voice was in luck: Persikov had overtired himself during recent days. At that moment he just happened to be resting in an armchair, gazing sluggishly and limply through red-ringed eyes and smoking. He could do no more. And for this reason it was even with a certain curiosity that he looked out of the window and saw Alfred Bronsky on the pavement. The professor immediately recognised the titled owner of the visiting-card by his pointed hat and notebook. Bronsky bowed gently and respectfully to the window.

'Oh, is it you?' asked the professor. He did not have the strength to get angry, and he even seemed curious as to what would happen next. Shielded by the window, he felt safe from Alfred. The permanent bowler hat in the street immediately turned an ear to Bronsky. The sweetest of smiles wreathed the latter's face.

'A pair of minutes, dear Professor,' began Bronsky, straining his voice from the pavement, 'just one little question and a purely zoological one. Will you allow me to put it?'

'Put it,' replied Persikov laconically and ironically, and thought: 'All the same, there's something American about this swine.'

'What can you say on behalf of chickens, dear Professor?' cried Bronsky, making a megaphone of his hands.

Persikov was astonished. He sat down on the window sill, then got off, pressed a button and shouted, poking his finger towards the window:

'Pankrat, let the one on the pavement in.'

When Bronsky appeared in the laboratory, Persikov extended his kindness to such an extent that he roared at him:

'Sit down!'

And Bronsky, smiling in delight, sat on a revolving stool.

'Please explain to me,' began Persikov, 'you write things in these newspapers of yours?'

'Exactly so,' replied Alfred respectfully.

'And so I find it incomprehensible how you can write, if you aren't even able to speak Russian. What's this "a pair of minutes" and "on behalf of chickens"? You probably meant to ask "regarding chickens"?'

Bronsky laughed feebly and respectfully:

'Valentin Petrovich makes the corrections.'

'And who is Valentin Petrovich?'

'The head of the literary section.'

'Well, alright. Anyway, I'm not a philologist. Your Petrovich aside. What precisely is it desirable for you to know regarding chickens?'

'In general, everything you can tell me, Professor.'

Here Bronsky armed himself with a pencil. Sparks of triumph flared up in Persikov's eyes.

'You've come to me to no purpose, I'm not a specialist on fowl. You would do best of all to go to Yemelyan Ivanovich Portugalov[11] in the I University. I personally know very little…'

Bronsky smiled in delight, making it clear that he understood the dear professor's joke. 'A joke – little!' he scribbled in his notebook.

'Anyway, if you're interested, as you wish. Chickens, or cristates… a genus of birds of the order *Gallinae*. Of the pheasant family…' began Persikov in a loud voice and looking not at Bronsky, but somewhere into the distance, where a thousand people were imagined before him… 'of the pheasant family… *Phasianidae*. They are birds with a fleshy cutaneous crest and two wattles beneath the lower jaw… hm… although, actually, there is sometimes just one in the middle of the chin… Well, what else then. Wings short and rounded. Tail of medium length, somewhat graduated, and even, I would say, roof-shaped, the middle feathers bent in a sickle shape… Pankrat… bring model No. 705, the cockerel in section, from the model room… but then you don't need that?… Pankrat, don't bring the model… I repeat, I'm not a specialist, go and see Portugalov. Well then, I am personally familiar with six kinds of chicken that live in the wild… hm… Portugalov knows more… in India and on the Malay archipelago. For example, the Banki cockerel or Kazintu, it's found in the Himalayan foothills, throughout India, in Assam, in Burma… The swallow-tailed cockerel or *Gallius varius* on Lombok, Sumbava and Flores. And on the island of Java there is the remarkable cockerel *Gallius eneus*, in south-east India I can

recommend to you the very beautiful Sonnerat's cockerel…
I'll show you a drawing later on. And as far as Ceylon is
concerned, on Ceylon we encounter Stanley's cockerel, it's
not found anywhere else.'

Bronsky sat with his eyes goggling and scribbled away.

'Can I tell you anything else?'

'I'd like to learn something regarding chicken diseases,'
whispered Alfred ever so softly.

'Hm, I'm not a specialist… ask Portugalov… But anyway…
Well. Tapeworms, flukes, itch-mites, red mange, poultry ticks,
chicken-lice or down-eater, fleas, chickens' cholera, croup-
diphtheritic inflammation of the mucous membranes…
Pneumonomycosis, tuberculosis, chicken mange… lots of
things are possible…' (sparks were leaping in Persikov's
eyes)… 'poisoning, by, for example, water-hemlock, tumours,
rickets, jaundice, rheumatism, the *Achorion schoenleinii*
fungus… a very interesting disease. On infection with it, small
spots resembling mould are formed on the comb…'

Bronsky wiped the sweat from his forehead with a coloured
handkerchief.

'And what then, in your opinion, Professor, is the cause of
the present catastrophe?'

'What catastrophe?'

'What, haven't you read about it, Professor?' said Bronsky
in surprise, and pulled out of his briefcase a crumpled sheet of
the newspaper *Izvestiya*.

'I don't read newspapers,' replied Persikov, and knitted his
brows.

'But why not, Professor?' asked Alfred gently.

'Because they write some rubbish or other,' replied Persikov
without a moment's thought.

'But what do you mean, Professor?' whispered Bronsky

softly, and opened out the sheet.

'What's this?' asked Persikov, and even got up from his seat. Now the sparks began to leap in Bronsky's eyes. With a sharp, lacquered finger he underlined a headline of the most incredible size across the entire page of the newspaper: 'Chicken Pestilence in the Republic'.

'What?' asked Persikov, shifting his spectacles onto his forehead...

CHAPTER SIX
Moscow in June 1928

It shone, lights danced, went out and flared up. On Teatralnaya Square there moved the white lamps of buses, the green lights of trams; above the former Muir and Mirrielees,[12] above its added tenth floor, there jumped a multicoloured electrical woman, throwing out letter by letter the multicoloured words 'Workers' credit'. On the square opposite the Bolshoi Theatre, where a multicoloured fountain played in the night-time, a crowd was jostling and humming. And above the Bolshoi Theatre a gigantic loudspeaker was howling:

'The anti-chicken vaccinations in the Lefortovo Veterinary Institute have produced brilliant results. The number of chickens' deaths for today has halved.'

Then the loudspeaker changed its tone, something growled inside it, above the theatre there flared up and faded a green stream, and the loudspeaker complained in a bass voice:

'An Emergency Commission has been formed for the struggle with the fowl plague, comprising the People's Commissar for Health, the People's Commissar for Agriculture, the Head of Animal Husbandry Comrade Byrd-Piggychuk, Professors Persikov and Portugalov... and Comrade Rabinovich!... New attempts at intervention...' – the loudspeaker chuckled and cried like a jackal – 'in connection with the fowl plague!'

Teatralny Passage, Neglinny Lane and the Lubyanka blazed with white and violet stripes, spurted rays, howled out signals, were wreathed in dust. Crowds of people clustered by the walls around the large sheets of announcements, illuminated by sharp, red reflectors:

'Under threat of the gravest punishment the population are

forbidden to use chicken meat and eggs in food. Private traders attempting to sell them in markets are subject to criminal prosecution and confiscation of all property. All citizens owning eggs must, as a matter of urgency, hand them in to regional police departments.'

On the screen on the roof of *The Workers' Newspaper* chickens lay in a pile right up to the sky, and greenish firemen, breaking up and sparkling, poured kerosene onto them from hoses. Then red waves moved around the screen, lifeless smoke swelled up and flew about in shreds, crawled in a stream, and a fiery inscription leapt out: 'Burning of chicken corpses on Khodynka'.

Like blind holes amidst the frenziedly blazing windows of shops that traded until three in the morning with two breaks for lunch and dinner gazed boarded-up windows under the signs: 'Eggs for sale. Quality guaranteed'. Very frequently, howling alarmingly, overtaking heavy buses, past policemen rushed hissing vehicles with the inscription: 'Moscow Health Department. Ambulance'.

'Someone else stuffed himself on rotten eggs,' went a rustling in the crowd.

In the Petrovsky Lines the world-famous Empire restaurant was radiant with green and orange lamps, and inside on the tables, by the portable telephones, lay cardboard signs, covered with liqueur stains: 'By order – omelette off. Fresh oysters available'.

In The Hermitage, where, like beads, Chinese lanterns burned dolefully in the lifeless, stifled greenery, on a stage that murdered one's eyes with its piercing light, the satirical songsters Shrams and Karmanchikov sang satirical songs composed by the poets Ardo and Arguyev:

Oh, mama, what will I do
Without eggs??…

and clattered their feet in a tap dance.

The theatre named after the late Vsevolod Meyerhold, who died, as is well known, in 1927 during a production of Pushkin's *Boris Godunov*, when the trapezes bearing naked boyars collapsed,[13] threw out a mobile electric sign of various colours, announcing the play by the writer Erendorg *The Chickens' Croaking* in a production by Meyerhold's pupil, Honoured Director of the Republic Cockterman. Nearby, in The Aquarium, iridescent with advertising lights and gleaming with the half-naked female body, in the greenery of the stage, to thunderous applause, the writer Lenivtsev's revue *The Chicken's Children* was on. While down Tverskaya, with little lamps on the sides of their faces, walked a string of circus donkeys, bearing shining posters. At the Korsh Theatre there is a revival of Rostand's *The Cockerel*[14].

The little boys selling newspapers growled and howled between the wheels of motors:

'Nightmare find in cellar! Poland prepares for nightmare war!! Professor Persikov's nightmare experiments!!'

In the former Nikitin's circus, in a brown, greasy ring smelling pleasantly of dung, the deathly pale clown Bom said to a Bim who was swollen in cellular dropsy:

'I know why you're so sad!'

'Why-ee?' asked Bim squeakily.

'You buried some eggs in the ground, and the police from Station 15 found them!'

'Ha-ha-ha-ha,' laughed the circus, such that the blood in one's veins froze joyfully and miserably, and beneath the old dome the trapezes and a cobweb stirred.

'U-up!' cried the clowns piercingly, and a well-fed white horse carried out a woman of wondrous beauty standing on elegant legs in a crimson leotard.

* * *

Looking at no one, noticing no one, replying to none of the nudges and quiet and tender invitations from prostitutes, Persikov, inspired and solitary, crowned with unexpected fame, was making his way along Mokhovaya towards the fiery clock by the Manège. Here, not looking about him, absorbed in his thoughts, he collided with an odd, old-fashioned man, jabbing his fingers most painfully right into the wooden holster of the revolver hanging on the man's belt.

'Oh, damn!' squeaked Persikov. 'Excuse me.'

'My apologies,' replied the oncoming man in an unpleasant voice, and somehow they disengaged themselves in the human mush. And the professor, making for Prechistenka, immediately forgot about the collision.

CHAPTER SEVEN
Faight

It is not known whether the Lefortovo veterinary inoculations really were any good, whether the Samara blockade detachments were efficient, whether the hard-boiled measures taken in relation to those buying up eggs in Kaluga and Voronezh were effective, or whether the Moscow Emergency Commission worked successfully, but it is well known that two weeks after Persikov's last meeting with Alfred, the Union of Republics was absolutely clean as regards chickens. Here and there in the yards of little provincial towns abandoned chicken feathers lay around, bringing tears to the eyes, and in the hospitals the last of the greedy were recovering, finishing with their bloody diarrhoea and vomiting. Fortunately, there were no more than a thousand human deaths in the entire Republic. No major disturbances ensued either. In Volokolamsk, it is true, a self-styled prophet tried to promote himself by announcing that the chicken murrain was caused by none other than the commissars, but he had no particular success. At the Volokolamsk market a few policemen taking chickens away from peasant women were beaten up, and some panes of glass were knocked out of the local post and telegraph office. Fortunately, the efficient Volokolamsk SPD took measures, as a result of which, firstly, the prophet disappeared without trace, and, secondly, glass was put in at the telegraph office.

Reaching in the north as far as Archangel and Syumkin Vyselok, the pestilence stopped on its own, for the reason that it had nowhere further to go – in the White Sea, as is well known, there are no chickens. It stopped at Vladivostok too, for further on was the ocean. In the distant south it died out and fell quiet somewhere on the burnt expanses of Ordubat, Dzhulfa and Karabulak, while in the west it was held up in an amazing way right on the Polish and Romanian borders. Perhaps it was the climate that was different there, or maybe the blockade cordon measures taken by neighbouring governments played a part, but it is a fact that the pestilence went no further. The foreign press noisily, greedily discussed a murrain unheard of in history, but the government of the Soviet republics, without creating any fuss, worked indefatigably. The Emergency Commission for the Struggle with Fowl Plague changed its name to the Emergency Commission for the Revival and Regeneration of Poultry-Farming in the Republic, having been supplemented by a new Emergency Triumvirate comprised of sixteen comrades. 'Volunchick'[15] was founded, in which Persikov and Portugalov took their places as honorary deputy presidents. In the newspapers, beneath their portraits, appeared the headlines: 'Mass Purchase of Eggs Abroad' and 'Mr Hughes Wants to Smash the Egg Campaign'.[16] Throughout the whole of Moscow resounded the venomous *feuilleton* by the journalist Kolechkin which concluded with the words: 'Don't hanker after our eggs, Mr Hughes – you've got your own!'

Professor Persikov had overworked and completely worn himself out in the last three weeks. The chicken events had knocked him out of his stride and loaded him with a double weight. For evenings on end he was obliged to work at sittings of the chicken commissions and from time to time to endure long conversations, sometimes with Alfred Bronsky, some-times with the mechanical fat man. Together with Professor Portugalov and *Privat-docent* Ivanov and Borngart he was obliged to dissect hens and subject them to microscopy in the search for the plague bacillus, and even to write in rough and ready fashion in the course of three evenings a pamphlet: 'On Changes in the Liver of Chickens in the Plague'.

Persikov worked without particular ardour in the field of chickens, which is understandable – his head was entirely filled with another matter, fundamental and important, the matter from which the chicken catastrophe had torn him, i.e. the red ray. Ruining the health that even before was damaged, snatching hours from sleep and food, sometimes not returning to Prechistenka, but falling asleep on the oilskin couch in the laboratory at the Institute, Persikov spent whole nights busy at the chamber and the microscope.

Around the end of July the rush quietened down somewhat. The business of the renamed commission took a turn towards normality, and Persikov returned to the work that had been disturbed. The microscopes were loaded with new preparations, beneath the ray in the chamber fish and frog-spawn matured at fabulous speed. Specially ordered lenses were brought by aeroplane from Königsberg, and in the final days of July, under Ivanov's supervision, technicians constructed two new large chambers in which the ray attained at its source the width of a cigarette packet and at its mouth a full metre. Persikov rubbed his hands in glee and began to prepare for some mysterious and complex experiments. First of all he came to an understanding on the telephone with the People's Commissar for Enlightenment, and the receiver croaked him the most courteous cooperation of every kind, and then, also on the telephone, Persikov called up Comrade Byrd-Piggychuk, Head of the Animal Husbandry Department of the Supreme Commission. Persikov met with the warmest attention on the part of Byrd. It was a matter of a large foreign order for Professor Persikov. Byrd said into the telephone that he would immediately telegraph Berlin and New York. After this there was an enquiry from the Kremlin as to how Persikov was getting on, and an important and affectionate voice asked whether Persikov needed an automobile.

'No, thank you. I prefer travelling by tram,' replied Persikov.

'But why so?' asked the mysterious voice, and laughed indulgently.

In general, everyone conversed with Persikov either with respect and awe, or else laughing affectionately, as if at a little, albeit sizeable, child.

'It's quicker,' replied Persikov, after which the resonant low bass replied into the telephone:

'Well, as you wish.'

Another week passed, and Persikov, distancing himself more and more from the abating chicken questions, immersed himself totally in the study of the ray. The sleepless nights and overtiredness made his head bright, somehow transparent and light. Red rings never left his eyes now, and Persikov spent almost every night at the Institute. On one occasion he abandoned his zoological refuge to give a talk in the enormous Cecila[17] Hall on Prechistenka about his ray and its effect on the ovule. This was a gigantic triumph for the eccentric zoologist. The clapping of hands in the columned hall resulted in something flaking off and falling down from the ceilings, and the hissing arc tubes flooded the black dinner jackets of the Cecilists and the white dresses of the women with light. On the stage, alongside the lectern, on a glass table there sat on a dish, breathing heavily and turning grey, a moist frog the size of a cat. Notes were thrown onto the stage. Among them were seven amorous ones, and Persikov tore them up. He was forcibly dragged out onto the stage by the President of the Cecila to take a bow. Persikov bowed irritably, his hands were sweaty, moist, and his black tie sat not beneath his chin, but behind his left ear. Before him in breath and mist were hundreds of yellow faces and white male chests, and suddenly the yellow holster of a pistol flashed by and disappeared somewhere behind a white column. Persikov noted it vaguely and forgot about it. But as he was leaving after the talk, descending the crimson stair carpet, he suddenly felt unwell. For a moment the bright chandelier in the vestibule was shrouded in black, and Persikov began to feel confused and rather nauseous… He had a burning sensation, and it seemed that blood was flowing stickily and hotly down his neck… And with a trembling hand the professor grabbed at the banister.

'Are you unwell, Vladimir Ipatyich?' alarmed voices flew at him from all sides.

'No, no,' replied Persikov, recovering, 'I'm simply overtired… yes… Allow me to have a glass of water.'

* * *

It was a very sunny day in August. It disturbed the professor, and so the blinds were lowered. One adjustable reflector on a stem threw a pencil of sharp light onto the glass table, piled with instruments and lenses. With the back of his revolving chair reclined, Persikov, exhausted, was smoking and looking through the strips of smoke with eyes that were dead from tiredness, yet contented, into the partially open door of the chamber where, slightly heating up the already stuffy and impure air of the laboratory, there quietly lay the red shaft of the ray.

Somebody knocked at the door.

'Well?' asked Persikov.

The door creaked softly, and in came Pankrat. He stood to attention and, paling in awe before the deity, spoke thus:

'Faight's 'ere, Mr Professor, for to see you.'

The semblance of a smile appeared on the scientist's cheeks. He narrowed his little eyes and pronounced:

'That's interesting. But I'm busy.'

'With an official document, 'e says, out of the Kremlin.'

'Fate with a document? A rare combination,' said Persikov, and added: 'Well then, let's have him in here then!'

'Yes, sir,' replied Pankrat, and disappeared out of the door like a grass snake.

A minute later it creaked again, and a man appeared on the threshold. Persikov creaked as he revolved, and stared over his shoulder at the visitor over the top of his spectacles. Persikov was too distant from life – he was not interested in it – but here the fundamental and main feature of the man who had entered was obvious even to Persikov. He was oddly old-fashioned. In 1919 this man would have been perfectly appropriate on the streets of the capital, he would have been tolerable in 1924, at its beginning, but in 1928 he was odd. At a time when even the most backward section of the proletariat – the bakers – went around in jackets, when it was rare in Moscow to see a service jacket – an old-fashioned costume, finally abandoned at the end of 1924 – the man who had entered was wearing a double-breasted, short leather coat, green trousers, puttees and lace-up shoes on his feet, and at his side a huge Mauser pistol of old construction in a battered yellow holster. The face of the man who had entered made the same impression on Persikov as it did on everyone – an extremely unpleasant impression. Small eyes looked at the whole world in astonishment, and at the same time confidently, there was something unduly free and easy in his short legs and flat feet. His face was shaved to a blue colour. Persikov frowned immediately. He wheezed pitilessly as he revolved and, no longer looking at the man who

55

had entered over the top of his spectacles, but through them, pronounced:

'You're here with a document? So where is it?'

The man who had entered was obviously stunned by what he had seen. In general, he was not much capable of confusion, but here he became confused. Judging by his eyes, he was struck first of all by the cabinet with twelve shelves which extended to the ceiling and was jam-packed with books. Then, of course, by the chambers, in which, as in Hell, there glimmered the crimson ray, swollen in the lenses. And in the semi-darkness, in the revolving chair, by the sharp needle of the ray that thrust out from the reflector, Persikov himself was odd and majestic enough. The newcomer fastened a gaze upon him in which sparks of respect clearly leapt through the self-confidence, he handed him no document, but said:

'I am Alexander Semyonovich Faight!'

'Well? So what?'

'I've been appointed head of "The Red Ray" model State Farm,' elucidated the newcomer.

'Well?'

'And now I've come to you, Comrade, with a secret memorandum.'

'I'd be interested to learn. In brief, if you can.' Persikov had become so unaccustomed to the word 'comrade' that, when he heard it now, it jarred. He became patently irritated.

The newcomer unbuttoned the breast of his coat and thrust out an official order, typed on magnificent thick paper. He proffered it to Persikov. And then he sat down without invitation on a revolving stool.

'Don't jog the table,' said Persikov with hatred.

The newcomer looked round in fright at the table, on the far edge of which, in a damp, dark aperture there shone lifelessly, like emeralds, some creature's eyes. A chill emanated from them.

As soon as Persikov had finished reading the document, he rose from the stool and rushed to the telephone. A few seconds later he was already saying hurriedly, and in an extreme degree of irritation:

'Forgive me… I cannot understand… How can it be? I… without my consent, advice… I mean, the devil knows what he'll do!!'

Here the stranger turned on the stool, extremely offended.

'My apologies,' he began, 'I am the hea –'

But Persikov waved his little hook at him and continued:

'Excuse me, I cannot understand… In conclusion, I categorically protest. I do not give my approval for experiments with eggs… Until I try them myself…'

Something was croaking and tapping in the receiver, and even from a distance it was clear that the voice in the receiver, indulgent, was speaking with a little child. It ended with a crimson Persikov hanging up the receiver with a crash and saying past it to the wall:

'I wash my hands of it.'

He returned to the table, picked the document up from it, read it through once from top to bottom over the top of his glasses, then from bottom to top through the glasses, and suddenly howled:

'Pankrat!'

Pankrat appeared in the doorway, as if he had come up through a trapdoor in an opera. Persikov glanced at him and barked:

'Get out, Pankrat!'

And Pankrat, without expressing the slightest astonishment on his face, vanished.

Then Persikov turned to the newcomer and began to speak:

'Be so kind, sir… I obey. It's none of my business. And it's of no interest to me either.'

The newcomer was not so much offended by the professor as astonished.

'My apologies,' he began, 'but you are a comrade?…'

'Why do you keep on saying "comrade"?…' mumbled Persikov sullenly, and fell silent.

'However' was written on Faight's face.

'My apolo –' he began.

'So then, please,' Persikov interrupted. 'Here's an arc lamp. By moving the ocular,' Persikov clicked the lid of the chamber, which resembled a photographic camera, 'you get from it a pencil of light, which you can concentrate by moving the lenses here, No. 1… and mirror, No. 2,' Persikov extinguished the ray, then turned it on again on the floor of the asbestos chamber, 'and you can set out anything you like on the floor in the ray and conduct experiments. Exceedingly simple, isn't it?'

Persikov meant to express irony and scorn, but the newcomer did not notice them, as he peered attentively into the chamber with shining little eyes.

'But I warn you,' continued Persikov, 'you shouldn't poke your hands into the ray, because, according to my observations, it causes the spread of epitheliomas… but unfortunately I have as yet been unable to establish whether or not they are malignant.'

Here the newcomer hid his hands adroitly behind his back, dropping his leather cap, and looked at the professor's hands. They were burned right through with iodine, and the right one was bandaged up at the wrist.

'But what about you, Professor?'

'You can buy rubber gloves at Schwabe's on Kuznetsky Bridge,' replied the professor irritably. 'I'm not obliged to worry about that.'

Here Persikov looked at the newcomer as though through a magnifying glass:

'Where have you sprung from? In general... why you?...'

Faight finally took great offence.

'My apolo –'

'I mean, you do need to know what it's all about!... Why have you latched onto this ray?...'

'Because it's a matter of national importance...'

'Ah-ha. National? Then... Pankrat!'

And when Pankrat appeared:

'Wait, I'll have a think.'

And Pankrat obediently vanished.

'What I can't understand is this:' said Persikov, 'why the need for such haste and secrecy?'

'Professor, you've really got me muddled up now,' replied Faight, 'you must know that the chickens have all died, down to the very last one.'

'And so what of it?' yelled Persikov, 'is it that you want to resurrect them instantly, or something? And why with the aid of a still unstudied ray?'

'Comrade Professor,' replied Faight, 'honestly, you're confusing me. I'm telling you it's essential for the state to regenerate its poultry-farming, because they're writing all sorts of vile things about us abroad. Yes.'

'And let them write...'

'Well, you know,' replied Faight enigmatically, and turned his head.

'Who, I should like to know, had the idea of raising chickens from eggs...'

'Me,' replied Faight.

'Aha… So, then… And why, might I learn? Where did you learn about the properties of the ray?'

'I was at your talk, professor.'

'I've not yet done anything with eggs!… I'm just getting ready!'

'Honest to God, it'll work out,' said Faight, suddenly persuasively and sincerely, 'your ray is so renowned, you could breed elephants if you wanted, not just chicks.'

'Do you know what,' said Persikov, 'you're not a zoologist, no? Pity… you'd make a very bold experimenter… Yes… only you risk… failure… and you're just taking up my time…'

'We'll return your chambers. How's that?'

'When?'

'When I've hatched out the first batch.'

'How confidently you say it! All right then. Pankrat!'

'I've got men with me,' said Faight, 'and an escort…'

By evening Persikov's laboratory had been orphaned… The tables had been emptied. Faight's men had taken away the three large chambers, leaving the professor only the first, his small one, with which he had begun his experiments.

The July twilight was coming on, greyness took possession of the Institute, it flowed down the corridors. In the laboratory could be heard monotonous steps – it was Persikov, measuring the large room from window to doors in the dark… It was an odd thing: on that evening an inexplicably mournful mood took possession of the people populating the Institute, and of the animals. The toads for some reason set up a particularly mournful concert and chirred ominously and in warning. Pankrat was obliged to hunt in the corridors for a grass snake which had left its chamber, and when he caught it, the grass snake looked as if it were ready to follow its nose anywhere, as

60

long as it got away.

In the deep twilight the ring of a bell was heard from Persikov's laboratory. Pankrat appeared on the threshold. And he saw a strange picture. The scientist was standing alone in the middle of the laboratory and looking at the tables. Pankrat coughed and froze.

'There, Pankrat,' said Persikov, and indicated the emptied table.

Pankrat was horrified. It seemed to him that the professor's eyes were tear-stained in the twilight. This was so unusual, so terrible.

'Yes, sir,' replied Pankrat piteously, and thought: 'Better if you yelled at me!'

'There,' repeated Persikov, and his lips quivered just like those of a child who for no apparent reason has had his favourite toy taken away from him.

'You know, dear Pankrat,' continued Persikov, turning away towards the window, 'my wife, who left fifteen years ago, she joined an operetta, and now it turns out she's died... That's the story, dear Pankrat... They've sent me a letter...'

The toads cried dolefully, and the twilight clothed the professor, there it is... the night. Moscow... somewhere outside the windows some white lamps were beginning to burn... Pankrat, embarrassed, was miserable, and stood to attention in fear...

'Go, Pankrat,' said the professor with difficulty, and waved his hand, 'go to bed, my dear chap, Pankrat, my friend.'

And the night set in. Pankrat ran out of the laboratory for some reason on tiptoe, ran to his cubby-hole, rummaged through the bits of cloth in the corner, pulled out from under them an opened bottle of Russian vodka and swigged down about a teacupful from it in one go. He helped it down with some bread and salt, and his eyes became a little more cheerful.

Late in the evening, already closer to midnight, Pankrat, sitting barefooted on a bench in the meagrely lit vestibule, was saying to the unsleeping bowler hat on duty, while scratching his chest under his cotton shirt:

'Better if 'e'd killed me, honest to Go...'

'Was he really crying?' asked the bowler hat curiously.

'Honest... to Go...' Pankrat assured him.

'The great scientist,' agreed the bowler hat, 'of course, a frog can't replace a wife.'

'No way,' agreed Pankrat.

Then he thought for a little and added:

'I been thinkin' of bringin' me old woman 'ere... why should she 'ave to sit in the countryside? Only she couldn't stick these reptiles, not for nothin'...'

'What can you say, the most awful filth,' agreed the bowler hat.

From the scientist's laboratory not a sound could be heard. And neither was there any light in it. There was no strip under the door.

CHAPTER EIGHT
The Business on the State Farm

There is positively no finer time than ripe August in, say, Smolensk Province. The summer of 1928 was, as is well known, the most excellent, with the rains on time in spring, with full, hot sun, with an excellent harvest... The apples on the former estate of the Sheremetyev family ripened... the woods were green, the squares of the fields lay yellow... Man becomes better too in the lap of nature. And Alexander Semyonovich would not have seemed as unpleasant as in the city. And he did not wear the offensive coat. His face was burnt to bronze, an unbuttoned cotton shirt showed a chest covered with the thickest growth of black hair, on his legs were sailcloth trousers. And his eyes became calmer and kinder.

Alexander Semyonovich ran animatedly down from the porch with its colonnade, whereon was nailed a sign beneath a star:

'RED RAY' STATE FARM

– and straight to the little truck which had brought the three black chambers under escort.

All day Alexander Semyonovich was busy with his assistants setting up the chambers in the former winter garden, the Sheremetyevs' hothouse... Towards evening all was ready. Under the glass ceiling a white frosted glass lamp had started to burn, the chambers were being set up on bricks, and the technician who had arrived with the chambers, after some flicking and turning of shining screws, lit up on the asbestos floor in the black boxes the red, mysterious ray.

Alexander Semyonovich was busy, he climbed onto the

ladder himself, checking the wires.

The next day the same little truck returned from the station and spat out three crates of magnificent smooth plywood with labels stuck all around them and with white inscriptions on a black background:

'*VORSICHT: EIER!!*'

'CAUTION: EGGS!!'

'Why ever have they sent so few?' thought Alexander Semyonovich in surprise, however he immediately got busy and began unpacking the eggs. The unpacking took place still in the same hothouse, and in it participated: Alexander Semyonovich himself, his unusually fat wife, Manya, the one-eyed former gardener of the former Sheremetyevs, now serving on the State Farm in the universal position of watchman, the guard, condemned to life on the State Farm, and the cleaner, Dunya. This is not Moscow, and everything here bore a more simple, friendly and family character. Alexander Semyonovich ordered things, casting occasional loving glances at the crates, which looked such a solid, compact gift in the gentle light of sunset from the upper panes of the hothouse. The guard, whose rifle dozed peacefully by the doors, was breaking open the clamps and metal edging with cutters. There was a lot of cracking... Dust fell. Alexander Semyonovich, with his sandals slapping, fussed about by the crates.

'Please, do be gentle,' he said to the guard. 'Careful. What's wrong with you, don't you see – eggs?'

'It's all right,' wheezed the provincial warrior, drilling away, 'just a minute...'

Tr-r-r... – and dust fell.

The eggs turned out to have been superbly packed: under the wooden lid was a layer of paraffin paper, then one of blotting-paper, then there followed a thick layer of wood shavings, then one of sawdust, and in that could be glimpsed the white tops of the eggs.

'Foreign packing,' said Alexander Semyonovich lovingly, rummaging in the sawdust, 'not like what we have here. Manya, be careful, you'll break them.'

'Alexander Semyonovich, you've gone soft in the head,' replied his wife, 'such valuable stuff, anyone'd think. Do you suppose I've never seen eggs before? Wow!... what big ones!'

'Foreign,' said Alexander Semyonovich, putting the eggs out onto a wooden table, 'not like our peasants' eggs... Probably all brahmas, the devil take them! German...'

'Of course,' confirmed the guard, admiring the eggs.

'But I don't understand why they're dirty,' said Alexander Semyonovich thoughtfully... 'Manya, you keep an eye on things. Let them carry on unloading, I'm going to the telephone.'

And Alexander Semyonovich set off for the telephone in the State Farm office across the yard.

In the evening in the laboratory of the Zoological Institute the telephone began rattling. Professor Persikov ruffled up his hair and went over to the apparatus.

'Well?' he asked.

'The provinces will be speaking with you in a moment,' the receiver responded, quietly and with a hissing sound, in a female voice.

'Well. Hello?' asked Persikov fastidiously into the black mouth of the telephone... Something clicked inside the latter, and then a distant male voice said anxiously into his ear:

'Should the eggs be washed, Professor?'

'What's that? What? What are you asking?' said Persikov in irritation. 'Where are you speaking from?'

'From Nikolskoye, Smolensk Province,' replied the receiver.

'I don't understand a thing. I don't know any Nikolskoye. Who is that?'

'Faight,' said the receiver sternly.

'What Faight? Oh, yes… it's you… so what is it you're asking?'

'Should they be washed?… I've been sent a batch of hens' eggs from abroad…'

'Well?'

'…and they're covered in some sort of muck…'

'You're confusing things… How can they be covered in "muck", as you put it? Well, of course, there may be a little… droppings dried on… or something else…'

'So they shouldn't be washed?'

'Of course there's no need… What, do you already want to load the eggs into the chambers?'

'I'm loading… Yes,' replied the receiver.

'Hm,' hemmed Persikov.

'Bye,' clanked the receiver, and fell quiet.

'"Bye",' Persikov repeated with hatred to *Privat-docent* Ivanov, 'how do you like that fellow, Pyotr Stepanovich?'

Ivanov burst out laughing.

'Was it him? I can just imagine what he'll cook up with those eggs.'

'B… b… b…' began Persikov bad-temperedly. 'Just you imagine, Pyotr Stepanovich… well, fine… it's quite possible that the ray will have the same effect on the deutoplasm of a hen's egg as on the reptiles' plasma. It's quite possible that he'll have chicks hatch out… But the thing is, neither you nor I can say what the chicks will be like… perhaps they're chicks that are no damned use. Perhaps they'll die in two days' time. Perhaps they can't be eaten! And can I guarantee that they'll stand up properly? Perhaps they have brittle bones.' Persikov grew heated, and waved his palm and bent his fingers.

'Perfectly true,' agreed Ivanov.

'Can you guarantee, Pyotr Stepanovich, that they'll breed successfully? Perhaps this fellow will raise sterile hens. Push them up to the size of a dog, but then wait until the Second Coming to get descendants from them.'

'It can't be guaranteed,' agreed Ivanov.

'And what familiarity,' Persikov went on upsetting himself, 'what glibness! And just take note, it is I that am charged with instructing this scoundrel,' Persikov indicated the document delivered by Faight (it was lying around on the experiment table)... 'and how am I to instruct him, this ignoramus, when I'm unable to say anything on this subject myself.'

'And could you not have refused?' asked Ivanov.

Persikov turned crimson, picked up the document and showed it to Ivanov. The latter read it through and gave an ironic smile.

'Mm – yes,' he said meaningfully.

'And just take note... I've been waiting for my order for two months, and I've not heard a word about it. Whereas he got the eggs straight away, and in general, cooperation of every kind...'

'He'll achieve damn all, Vladimir Ipatyich. And it will simply end with the chambers being returned to you.'

'If only that would happen soon, because they're holding up my experiments, you know.'

'Now that is a nuisance. I've got everything ready.'

'Have you received the protective suits?'

'Yes, today.'

Persikov became a little less upset and more animated.

'Aha... I think this is what we'll do. We'll close the doors of

67

the operating theatre tight, and we'll open the window…'

'Of course,' agreed Ivanov.

'Three helmets?'

'Three. Yes.'

'Well, then… So, you and I, and we can nominate one of the students. We'll give him the third helmet.'

'Grinmut, perhaps.'

'Is that the one you now have working on the sala-manders?… hm… he's all right… although in the spring, if you please, he couldn't say how the swim-bladder of the gymnodontes was structured,' added Persikov rancorously.

'No, he's all right… He's a good student,' Ivanov interceded.

'We'll even have to go one night without sleep,' continued Persikov, 'only the thing is this, Pyotr Stepanovich, you check the gas, or else the devil knows, these "Volunchem" people of theirs. They might send some filth or other.'

'No, no,' and Ivanov began waving his hands, 'I've already tried it, yesterday. You've got to give them credit, Vladimir Ipatyich, it's superb gas.'

'Who did you try it on?'

'Common toads. You let out a jet and they die instantly. Yes, and this is what we'll do as well, Vladimir Ipatyich. You write a memorandum to the SPD for them to send you an electric revolver.'

'But I don't know how to handle it.'

'I take it upon myself,' replied Ivanov, 'we fired one on the River Klyazma for fun… there was an SPD man living there with me… It's a remarkable thing. And extraordinarily simple… It kills without a sound at about a hundred paces, and outright. We shot at crows… I don't think gas is even necessary.'

'Hm... it's a clever idea... Very.' Persikov went into the corner, picked up the receiver and croaked:

'Give me the... what's it called... Lubyanka...'

* * *

The days were hot in the extreme. Above the fields the transparent, fatty, intense heat could clearly be seen undulating. Yet the nights were wondrous, deceptive, green. The moon shone and covered the former estate of the Sheremetyevs in such beauty that it cannot be expressed. The palace-cum-State Farm gleamed as if made of sugar, the shadows trembled in the park, while the ponds divided into two differently coloured halves – a slanting column of moonlight, and a half of bottomless darkness. In the spots of moon *Izvestiya* could be read easily, with the exception of the chess section, set in small nonpareil. But on such nights, naturally, nobody was reading *Izvestiya*. Dunya the cleaner was to be found in the grove beyond the State Farm, and there too was to be found, in consequence of a coincidence, the red-whiskered driver of the battered State Farm truck. What they did there is unknown. They took shelter in the precarious shade of an elm, directly on top of the driver's wide-spread leather coat. A lamp burned in the kitchen, two market-gardeners had dinner there, while Madame Faight sat in a white house-coat on the columned veranda and dreamed, gazing at that beauty, the moon.

At ten o'clock in the evening, when the sounds had died away in the village of Finalevka that lay beyond the State Farm, the idyllic landscape resounded to the charming, gentle sounds of a flute. It is unthinkable to express how appropriate they were above the groves and former columns of the

Sheremetyev palace. Delicate Liza from *The Queen of Spades*[18] mingled her voice in a duet with the voice of the passionate Polina and flew off into the lunar heights, like a vision of an old, yet endlessly dear regime, enchanting to the point of tears.

They die away... They die away...

whistled the flute, modulating and sighing.

The groves fell still, and Dunya, baneful, like a sylvan mermaid, listened with her cheek pressed up against the rough, ginger and manly cheek of the driver.

'Blows a good pipe though, the son of a bitch,' said the driver, putting his manly arm around Dunya's waist.

The flute was played by the head of the State Farm, Alexander Semyonovich Faight himself, and he played, you have to give him his due, superbly. The fact was that the flute was once Alexander Semyonovich's speciality. Right up until 1917 he worked in the famous concert ensemble of the maestro Roosterov, which every evening in the town of Odessa filled the foyer of the cosy picture-house Magical Daydreams with elegant sounds. But the great year of 1917, which broke the career of many in two, led Alexander Semyonovich down new paths as well. He abandoned Magical Daydreams and the dusty, starry satin in the foyer, and threw himself into the open sea of war and revolution, exchanging his flute for a destructive Mauser. For a long time he was tossed about on the waves and repeatedly thrown out, with a splash, now in the Crimea, now in Moscow, now in Turkestan, now even in Vladivostok. The revolution was just the thing that was needed to bring Alexander Semyonovich out fully. It transpired that this man was positively great and, of course, it was not for him to sit in the foyer of Daydreams. Without going into lengthy detail, we will say that the preceding year of 1927 and the beginning of 1928 found Alexander Semyonovich in Turkestan, where, firstly, he edited a huge politico-literary newspaper, and then, as a local member of the Supreme Communal Economic Commission, became renowned for his astonishing work on the irrigation of the Turkestan region. In 1928 Faight arrived in Moscow and was given a well-earned rest. The Supreme Commission of the organisation, whose card this provincially old-fashioned man carried with honour in his pocket, appraised him and appointed him to a peaceful and honourable post. Alas! Alas! To the Republic's cost Alexander Semyonovich's seething brain did not switch off, in Moscow Faight ran into Persikov's invention, and in the rooms of Red Paris on Tverskaya Street Alexander Semyonovich gave birth to the idea of how, with the help of Persikov's ray, the Republic's chickens could be reborn in the course of a month. Faight was received in the Kremlin, the Kremlin concurred with him, and Faight came with the thick document to see the eccentric zoologist.

The concert above the glassy waters and the groves and the park was already nearing its end when suddenly something occurred to cut it short prematurely. Namely, the dogs in Finalevka, who, judging by the time, ought to have been asleep already, suddenly started up an intolerable barking, which gradually turned into the most excruciating general howling. The howling spread out and flew across the fields, and the howling was suddenly answered by the harsh concert of the million voices of the frogs on the ponds. All this was so horrible, that it even seemed for a moment as if the mysterious, bewitching night had grown dim.

Alexander Semyonovich left his flute and went out onto the veranda.

'Manya. Do you hear? Those damned dogs… what do you think they're going crazy about?'

'How should I know?' replied Manya, gazing at the moon.

'You know what, Manyechka, let's go and have a little look at the eggs,' suggested Alexander Semyonovich.

'I swear to God, Alexander Semyonovich, you've gone completely soft with your eggs and your chicks. Relax a bit.'

'No, Manyechka, let's go.'

In the hothouse a bright lamp was burning. Dunya arrived too, with a burning face and shining eyes. Alexander Semyonovich gently opened the control panes, and they all began to look inside the chambers. In straight rows on the white asbestos floor lay bright-red eggs with spots scattered all over them, the chambers were soundless… and the 15,000 candle-power lamp above hissed quietly…

'Oh, am I going to hatch out those little chicks!' said Alexander Semyonovich enthusiastically, looking in now from the side through the control slits, now from above through the wide ventilation apertures. 'You'll see… What? You think I won't?'

'You know what, Alexander Semyonovich,' said Dunya with a smile, 'the peasants in Finalevka said you were the Antichrist. They say your eggs are the devil's. It's a sin to hatch them out with a machine. They wanted to kill you.'

Alexander Semyonovich gave a start and turned to his wife. His face had gone yellow.

'Well, what do you say to that? That's the people for you! Well, what can you do with people like that? Eh? Manyechka, we'll have to do a meeting for them… I'll call in some party workers from the district town. I'll make a speech to them myself. In general, we'll have to do a bit of work here… It's a backward sort of place as it stands…'

'The Dark Ages,' said the guard, who had settled himself on his greatcoat by the hothouse door.

The following day was marked by the most dreadful and inexplicable occurrences. In the morning, at the very first light of the sun, the groves, which usually greeted the day-star with the unceasing and powerful chattering of birds, met it with complete silence. This was noticed by absolutely everyone. Like before a thunderstorm. But there was no sign of any thunderstorm. Conversations on the State Farm took on a strange and ambiguous tone for Alexander Semyonovich, and in particular because, from what was said by the peasant nicknamed Goat's Crop, a well-known troublemaker and sage from Finalevka, it became known that all the birds had apparently gathered into flocks and at dawn had cleared off somewhere away from Sheremetyevo, to the north, which was simply stupid. Alexander Semyonovich got very upset and wasted the whole day on ringing up the Committee in Rookovka. They promised in two days or so to send Alexander Semyonovich speakers on two topics – the international situation and the question of Volunchick.

The evening was not without surprises either. If in the morning the groves had fallen silent, showing quite clearly how suspiciously unpleasant silence is among trees, if at noon the sparrows had cleared off somewhere from the State Farm yard, then by the evening the pond at Sheremetyevo had fallen silent. This was truly astonishing, as everyone for forty kilometres around knew supremely well the renowned chattering of the Sheremetyevs' frogs. But now it was as if they had died out. Not a single voice carried from the pond, and the sedge stood soundlessly. It must be admitted that Alexander Semyonovich was as upset as could be. People had begun to talk about these occurrences, and to talk in the most

73

unpleasant way, i.e. behind Alexander Semyonovich's back.

'It really is strange,' said Alexander Semyonovich to his wife at dinner, 'I can't understand why those birds found it necessary to fly away.'

'How should I know?' replied Manya. 'Perhaps away from your ray?'

'Oh, Manya, you're the most common or garden fool,' replied Alexander Semyonovich, throwing down his spoon, 'you're like the peasants. What has the ray got to do with it?'

'I don't know. Leave me alone.'

In the evening the third surprise occurred – the dogs again began howling in Finalevka, and how! Above the moonlit fields there hung an unbroken groaning, baleful, miserable groans.

Alexander Semyonovich was somewhat recompensed by another surprise, but this time a pleasant one, in the hothouse to be precise. In the chambers an incessant tapping inside the red eggs began to be heard. 'Tack... tack... tack... tack...' came the tapping, now in one, now in another, now in a third egg.

The tapping in the eggs was the tapping of triumph for Alexander Semyonovich. The strange occurrences in the grove and at the pond were immediately forgotten. Everyone gathered in the hothouse: Manya, Dunya, the watchman and the guard, who left his rifle by the door.

'Well, then? What do you say?' asked Alexander Semyonovich jubilantly. Everyone bent their ears curiously to the doors of the first chamber.

'It's them tapping with their beaks, the chicks,' continued Alexander Semyonovich, beaming. 'Can you say I won't hatch out the chicks? No, my friends.' And in an excess of emotion he slapped the guard on the shoulder. 'I'll hatch out such chicks, you'll be speechless. Now I want you to keep your wits about you,' he added sternly. 'The moment they begin hatching, let me know straight away.'

'All right,' chorused the watchman, Dunya and the guard.

'Tock… tock… tock…' in the first chamber things were beginning to come to the boil first in one, then in another egg. Indeed, the picture of new life being born before their eyes within a thin, reflective skin was so interesting, that the entire company sat for a long time yet on the upturned empty crates, watching the crimson eggs ripening in the mysterious, glimmering light. They dispersed to bed quite late, when the greenish night had spilled over the State Farm and its surroundings. The night was mysterious and, it could be said, even terrible, probably because its total silence was broken by the unmotivated, extremely miserable and whining howl of the dogs that kept on starting up in Finalevka. Why the damned hounds were going crazy is quite unknown.

Something unpleasant awaited Alexander Semyonovich in the morning. The guard was extremely embarrassed, kept putting his hands to his heart, vowed and swore that he had not been asleep, but had noticed nothing.

'It's incomprehensible,' the guard claimed, 'I'm not to blame, Comrade Faight.'

'Thank you, from the bottom of my heart, I'm grateful,' Alexander Semyonovich berated him, 'what do you think, Comrade? Why were you posted here? To keep watch. So you tell me, then, where have they got to? They've hatched, haven't they? That means they've got away. That means you left the door open, and you went off somewhere yourself too. I want the chicks found!'

'There's nowhere for me to go. Don't I know my job, then?' the warrior finally took offence. 'Why are you reproaching me for nothing, Comrade Faight?'

'Where on earth have they got to?'

'How am I to know?' the warrior finally raged, 'am I supposed to be standing watch over them? Why am I posted? To see that nobody pinches the chambers, and I'm carrying out my duty. There are your chambers. And I'm not required by law to try and catch your chicks. Who knows what chicks you might have hatching out, perhaps you won't catch them up on a bike!'

Alexander Semyonovich was rather taken aback, muttered something else and fell into a state of astonishment. It was indeed a strange business. In the first chamber, which had been loaded first of all, the two eggs positioned by the very base of the ray, proved to be broken open. And one of them had even rolled away to one side. The shell was lying on the asbestos floor, in the ray.

'The devil knows,' mumbled Alexander Semyonovich, 'the windows are locked, they can't have flown off through the roof, can they?'

He craned his neck and looked up to where there were several large holes in the glass covering of the roof.

'What are you talking about, Alexander Semyonovich,' said Dunya in extreme surprise, 'the chicks won't go flying about. They're here somewhere... Chick... chick... chick...' she began calling and looking into the corners of the hothouse, where there stood dusty flowerpots, planks of some sort and junk. But no chicks responded from anywhere.

The entire administrative staff ran about the State Farm yard for two hours or so in search of the sprightly chicks, but did not find anything anywhere. The day passed in extreme excitement. The guard on the chambers was increased with the addition of the watchman, and the latter was given the strictest instructions to look in at the windows of the chambers every quarter of an hour and, at the first hint of anything, to call Alexander Semyonovich. The guard sat frowning by the doors, holding his rifle between his knees. Alexander Semyonovich quite wore himself out with all the fuss and had lunch only after it had gone one in the afternoon. After lunch he had an hour's sleep in the cool shade on Sheremetyev's former ottoman, drank his fill of the State Farm's rusk kvass, visited the hothouse and satisfied himself that everything there was now in complete order. The old watchman lay on his stomach on some matting and, blinking, gazed into the control glass of the first chamber. The guard was awake and had not moved away from the doors.

But there was news too: the eggs in the third chamber, loaded last of all, had begun somehow to make a lip-smacking, lisping noise, as if someone were sobbing inside them.

'Ooh, they're ripening,' said Alexander Semyonovich, 'that's ripening, now I can see. Seen it?' he addressed the watchman.

'Yes, it's remarkable,' replied the latter, shaking his head and in an utterly ambiguous tone.

Alexander Semyonovich sat for a little by the chambers, but nothing hatched out while he was there, he rose from his squatting position, stretched his legs and announced that he was not going anywhere away from the estate, but would only be going to the pond to swim, and that, if anything happened, he was to be summoned immediately. He ran off to the bedroom in the palace where there stood two narrow sprung beds with crumpled bedclothes and where on the floor were piled up a heap of green apples and mountains of millet, prepared for the future broods, and armed himself with a fluffy towel, but after a moment's thought took his flute with him as well, so as to play a little at leisure over the untroubled waters. He ran out cheerily from the palace, cut across the State Farm

77

yard and went down a willow walk in the direction of the pond. Faight walked cheerily, swinging the towel and holding the flute under his arm. The sky poured the heat out through the willows, and his body ached and begged to get into the water. On Faight's right hand there began a thicket of burdock, into which he spat as he was passing. And at once in the depths of the tangled mess a rustling was heard, as if somebody had set off dragging a log. Feeling a fleeting, unpleasant gnawing in his heart, Alexander Semyonovich turned his head towards the thicket and looked in surprise. For two days already the pond had not made any sound. The rustling ceased, above the burdock there was an attractive glimpse of the smooth waters of the pond and the grey roof of the little bathing-hut. Several dragonflies sped by in front of Alexander Semyonovich. He already meant to turn towards the wooden planking, when suddenly the rustling in the greenery was repeated, and it was joined by a brief hoarse noise, as if oil and steam had seeped out of a steam engine. Alexander Semyonovich pricked up his ears and began peering into the blank wall of the thicket of weeds.

'Alexander Semyonovich,' the voice of Faight's wife rang out at that moment, and her white blouse was glimpsed, then disappeared, but was glimpsed once more in the raspberry-canes. 'Wait, I'll come for a swim as well.'

His wife was hurrying towards the pond, but Alexander Semyonovich made her no reply, being entirely riveted to the burdock. A greyish and olive log began to rise out of the thicket, growing before his eyes. There were wet, yellowish blotches of some kind, as it seemed to Alexander Semyonovich, scattered all over the log. It began to stretch out, bending and moving, and it stretched out so high that it overtook a short, gnarled willow... Then the top of the log broke away, bent down a little, and above Alexander Semyonovich there appeared something reminiscent in height of a Moscow electricity pole. Only this something was about three times as thick as a pole and much more beautiful thanks to a tattoo of scales. Without yet understanding anything, but already turning cold, Alexander Semyonovich glanced at the top of the dreadful pole, and the heart within him stopped its beating for several seconds. It seemed to him that frost had struck unexpectedly on an August day, and before his eyes twilight had fallen, as though he were looking at the sun through summer trousers.

At the top end of the log there turned out to be a head. It was flattened, sharpened and adorned with a round yellow blotch against an olive background. Devoid of eyelids, the open, icy and narrow eyes sat in the roof of the head, and in those eyes there glimmered a quite unprecedented malice. The head made a movement as though it had pecked at the air, the entire pole was drawn into the burdock, and just the eyes alone remained and, unblinking, looked at Alexander Semyonovich. The latter, covered in sticky sweat, pronounced four words, utterly improbable and elicited by maddening terror. To such a degree were those eyes amidst the leaves attractive.

'What kind of joke...'

Then he remembered that fakirs... yes... yes... India... a woven basket and a picture... They charm.

The head arched up once more, and the trunk began to emerge too. Alexander Semyonovich brought the flute up to his lips, gave a hoarse squeak and, gasping for breath at every second, started to play the waltz from *Eugene Onegin*[19]. The eyes in the greenery immediately began to burn with an implacable hatred for that opera.

'What, are you out of your mind, playing in this heat?'
Manya's cheerful voice rang out, and out of the corner of his
eye Alexander Semyonovich caught sight of a white spot
somewhere on the right.

Then a heart-rending scream pierced the entire State Farm,
spread out and took off, while the waltz started jumping, as if it
had a broken leg. The head darted forward from the greenery,
its eyes abandoned Alexander Semyonovich, releasing his soul
for repentance. A snake of approximately thirty feet and the
thickness of a man leapt like a spring out of the burdock.
A cloud of dust spurted from the road and the waltz ended.
The snake rushed past the head of the State Farm straight to
where the white blouse was on the road. Faight saw it quite
distinctly: Manya became yellowy-white, and her long hair
stood up like wire a foot above her head. Before Faight's eyes,
the snake, for a moment opening wide its jaws, from which
something resembling a fork dived out, used its teeth to grab
Manya, who was subsiding into the dust, by the shoulder, so
that it jerked her up a yard above the ground. Then Manya
repeated the piercing pre-death cry. The snake wound itself
up into a ten-foot screw, its tail swept up a dust-storm, and it
began squeezing Manya to death. The latter did not utter
another sound, and Faight only heard her bones cracking.
Manya's head flew up high above the ground, pressing
tenderly against the snake's cheek. Blood splashed out of
Manya's mouth, a broken arm slipped out and from under
the fingernails there spurted little fountains of blood. Then
the snake, dislocating its jaws, opened its mouth wide and in
one go fitted its own head onto Manya's and began slipping
down onto her like a glove onto a finger. There was such hot
breath emanating from the snake in all directions that it
touched Faight's face, while its tail almost swept him from the

road in acrid dust. It was at this point that Faight's hair turned white. First the left, and then the right side of his head, black as coal, was covered in silver. In mortal nausea he finally tore himself away from the road and, seeing nothing and no one, filling the surroundings with a wild howling, he started running…

CHAPTER NINE
Living Mush

Schukin, the State Political Directorate's agent at Dugino station, was a very courageous man. He said pensively to his comrade, red-haired Polaitis:

'Well, let's go, then. Eh? Let's have the motorbike,' then after a short silence, addressing the man sitting on a bench, he added: 'Put the flute down.'

Yet the shaking, white-haired man on the bench in the Dugino SPD building did not put the flute down, but began crying and mumbling. Then Schukin and Polaitis realised the flute had to be removed. The fingers were stuck to it. Schukin, who was notable for his enormous strength, almost that of a circus performer, started bending back finger after finger, until he had bent them all back. Then the flute was put on the table.

This was early on the sunny morning of the day following Manya's death.

'You'll come with us,' said Schukin, addressing Alexander Semyonovich, 'you'll show us where and what.' But Faight moved away from him in horror and hid himself with his arms, as if from a terrible vision.

'You need to show us,' added Polaitis sternly.

'No, leave him. The man's not himself, you can see.'

'Send me to Moscow,' requested Alexander Semyonovich, crying.

'You won't return to the State Farm at all, then?'

But instead of replying, Faight again shielded himself with his arms, and horror flowed from his eyes.

'Well, all right,' decided Schukin, 'you really haven't got the strength... I can see. An express will be leaving soon, you go with it.'

Then, while the station watchman was giving Alexander Semyonovich a drink of water, and the latter's teeth were chattering on the blue, dented mug, Schukin and Polaitis had a conference. Polaitis supposed that none of this had happened at all, that Faight was quite simply insane and had had a terrible hallucination. Whereas Schukin was inclined towards the notion that a boa constrictor had escaped from the town of Rookovka, where at the present time there was a touring circus. Hearing their sceptical whispering, Faight half stood up. He came to his senses somewhat and said, spreading his arms like a biblical prophet:

'Listen to me. Listen. Why, oh why do you not believe me? It was there. Where's my wife, then?'

Schukin became silent and serious and immediately sent some sort of telegram to Rookovka. On Schukin's instructions, a third agent began to be with Alexander Semyonovich continually and was to accompany him to Moscow. But Schukin and Polaitis began preparing for the expedition. They had only one electric revolver, but even this was already a pretty good defence. The fifty-round model of 1927, the pride of French technology for fighting at close quarters, had a range of only one hundred paces, but offered a field of two metres in diameter, and within this field it killed any living thing outright. It was very difficult to miss. Schukin put on the shiny electric toy, and Polaitis an ordinary twenty-five-round sub-machine gun, he took some cartridge belts, and on a single motorcycle, through the morning cold and dew, they rolled off down the highway towards the State Farm. The motorcycle rattled out the twenty kilometres separating the station from the State Farm in a quarter of an hour (Faight had walked all night, continually hiding, in fits of mortal terror, in the grass on the roadside), and when the sun had begun to get significantly hot, on the knoll at the foot of which there wound the little River Top, the confectionery palace with the columns peeped out amidst the greenery. A deathly hush hung all around. Right by the approach to the State Farm the agents overtook a peasant on a cart. He was plodding along unhurriedly, loaded up with sacks of some kind, and was soon left behind. The motorcycle ran over the bridge, and Polaitis sounded the horn to summon somebody. But nobody responded anywhere, with the exception of the far-off, frenzied dogs in Finalevka. The motorcycle, slowing down, approached the gates bearing lions that had turned green. The dusty agents in yellow gaiters jumped off, chained and padlocked the vehicle to the transom of the railings and entered the yard. They were struck by the quiet.

'Hey, is anybody here?' called Schukin loudly.

But nobody responded to his bass. The agents walked around the yard, becoming more and more surprised. Polaitis frowned. Schukin began to look serious, furrowing his blond brows more and more. They glanced through the closed window into the kitchen and saw there was nobody there, but the entire floor was covered with splinters of white crockery.

'You know, something really has happened here. I can see it now. A catastrophe,' pronounced Polaitis.

'Hey, is anybody there? Hey!' shouted Schukin, but he was answered only by the echo beneath the vaults of the kitchen.

'The devil knows!' grumbled Schukin. 'I mean, it couldn't have gobbled them all up at once... They must have run off. We'll go into the house.'

The door of the palace with the columned veranda was wide open, and inside it was quite empty. The agents even went into the mezzanine, knocking and opening all the doors, but they achieved absolutely nothing and through the deserted porch they came out once more into the yard.

'We'll go round the outside. To the hothouses,' ordered Schukin, 'we'll give it a good going over, and then we'll be able to telephone.'

The agents set off along the brick pathway, passing by the flower-beds, to the rear yard, they cut across it and saw the shining panes of the hothouse.

'Just hang on,' remarked Schukin in a whisper, and unfastened the revolver from his belt. Polaitis pricked up his ears and brought the sub-machine gun down. A terrible and very shrill sound extended through the hothouse and some way beyond it. It was as if a steam engine were hissing somewhere. 'Zaoo-zaoo... zaoo-zaoo... s-s-s-s-s...' the hot-house hissed.

'Right now, careful,' whispered Schukin, and, trying to stop their heels clicking, the agents moved right up to the panes and peeped into the hothouse.

Polaitis immediately recoiled, and his face became pale. Schukin opened his mouth and froze with the revolver in his hand.

The entire hothouse was alive, like worm-ridden mush. Curling up into balls and uncurling, hissing and unrolling, groping about and shaking their heads, over the floor of the hothouse crawled enormous snakes. Broken shell lay around on the floor and crunched beneath their bodies. Above, an electric lamp of enormous power burned wanly, and as a result the whole interior of the hothouse was lit with a strange cinematographic light. On the floor there protruded three dark, enormous boxes, like cameras; two of them, pushed aside and tilted, had grown dim, but in the third there burned a small, densely crimson spot of light. Snakes of all sizes crawled along the cables, climbed up the transoms of the window frames, clambered out through apertures in the roof. On the electric lamp itself hung an utterly black, mottled snake several metres long, and its head rocked by the lamp like a pendulum. Rattles of some kind were jangling in the hissing, from the hothouse there came a strange, putrefactive smell, as if from a pond. And the agents could still vaguely make out piles of white eggs, lying around in dusty corners, and a strange, gigantic, lanky bird, which lay motionless by the chambers, and the corpse of a man in grey by the door, alongside a rifle.

'Back,' cried Schukin, and began moving backwards, pressing Polaitis away with his left hand and raising the revolver with his right. He had time to fire some nine times, fizzing and throwing out greenish lightning about the hothouse. The sound swelled terribly, and in response to Schukin's firing the entire hothouse went into frenzied motion, and flat heads began to appear in every hole. Thunder began at once to leap around the whole State Farm and its reflections to play on the walls. 'Chack-chack-chack-tack,' fired Polaitis, retreating backwards. A terrible, four-footed rustling was heard from behind, and Polaitis suddenly gave a terrible cry as he fell on his face. A creature on splayed feet, browny-green in colour, with a huge, sharp head and a ridged tail, resembling a lizard of terrible dimensions, had rolled out from around the corner of a shed and, savagely biting through Polaitis' leg, had toppled him to the ground.

'Help,' cried Polaitis, and immediately his left arm was snapped up and crunched by a pair of jaws; with his right arm, which he tried in vain to raise, he dragged his revolver over the ground. Schukin turned round and began to rush about. He managed to fire once, but bore way off to the side, as he was afraid of killing his comrade. He fired a second time in the direction of the hothouse, because from there, amongst small snakes' heads, one enormous one was thrust out, olive-coloured, and the trunk leapt out straight towards him. With this shot he killed the gigantic snake and again, jumping and circling around Polaitis, who was already half-dead in the crocodile's jaws, he tried to choose a place he could fire at to kill the terrible reptile without touching the agent. He finally succeeded in this. There were two claps from the electric revolver, which illuminated all around with a greenish light, and the crocodile jumped and stretched out dead, releasing Polaitis. Blood flowed from the latter's sleeve, flowed from his mouth, and, putting his weight on his healthy right arm, he trailed his broken left leg. The light was dying away in his eyes…

'Schukin… run…' he mumbled, sobbing.

Schukin fired several times in the direction of the hothouse, where several panes of glass flew out. But a huge spring, olive-coloured and flexible, having slipped out of a basement window, slid across the yard, occupying the whole of it with its ten-metre body, and in a moment wrapped itself around Schukin's legs from behind. He was tossed down onto the ground, and the shining revolver leapt away to one side. Schukin gave a mighty cry, then choked, then the coils concealed him completely, apart from his head. A coil passed once across his head, tearing off its scalp, and the head cracked. Not one more shot was heard on the State Farm. Everything was smothered by a hissing sound that drowned everything out. And in reply to it, on the wind, from very far away in Finalevka was carried a howling, but it was now no longer possible to make out whose howling it was, canine or human.

CHAPTER TEN
Catastrophe

In the night, in the editorial office of the newspaper *Izvestiya* the lamps were burning brightly, and on a lead table the fat editor was making up the second type-page with telegrams 'Across the Union of Republics'. One galley proof caught his eye, he peered at it through his pince-nez and burst into chuckles, gathered the proofreaders from the proofreading room and the maker-up around him and showed this galley proof to everyone. On a narrow little strip of damp paper was printed:

'Rookovka. Smolensk Province. There has appeared in the district a chicken the size of a horse and it kicks like a steed. Instead of a tail it has bourgeois ladies' feathers.'

The typesetters chuckled terribly.

'In my time,' began the editor, giggling in bold, 'when I worked on Vanya Sytin's *Russian Word*[20], people used to drink themselves into seeing elephants. That's true. But now, it appears, into seeing ostriches.'

The typesetters chuckled.

'But that's right, isn't it, an ostrich,' began the maker-up, 'what shall we put, then, Ivan Vonifatyevich?'

'What's the matter, have you gone crazy?' replied the editor. 'I'm surprised at the secretary letting it through – it's just a drunken telegram.'

'They had a good time, that's for sure,' agreed the typesetters, and the maker-up removed the report about the ostrich from the table.

And so *Izvestiya* came out on the next day containing, as usual, masses of interesting material, but without any allusions whatsoever to the Rookovka ostrich. *Privat-docent* Ivanov, reading *Izvestiya* thoroughly in his laboratory, folded the sheet up, yawned, pronounced 'nothing of interest', and started putting on a white coat. After a little while the burners in his laboratory began to burn and the frogs began to croak. In Professor Persikov's laboratory, though, there was a commotion. A frightened Pankrat was there and standing to attention.

'Understood... yes, sir,' he said.

Persikov handed him a package sealed with sealing wax, saying:

'You'll go straight to the Department of Animal Husbandry to this head of theirs, Byrd, and tell him straight that he's a swine. Tell him that I, Professor Persikov, said exactly that. And give him the package.'

'Nice job,' thought the pale Pankrat, and cleared off with the package.

Persikov was raging.

'It's the devil knows what,' he whined, walking about the laboratory and rubbing his gloved hands, 'it's unheard-of mockery at my expense and the expense of zoology. These damned hens' eggs are brought in heaps, while I can't get hold of what's required for two months. As if it's a long way to America! Constant commotion, constant outrage.' He started counting on his fingers: 'The hunting... well, ten days at the most, well, all right – fifteen... well, all right, twenty, and the flight across – two days, from London to Berlin – a day... From Berlin to us – six hours... an indescribable outrage...'

He threw himself savagely upon the telephone and began making a call somewhere.

In his laboratory everything was ready for some mysterious and highly dangerous experiments, paper lay cut up into strips for sealing the doors, diving helmets with breathing tubes and several cylinders lay, shining like mercury, labelled 'Volunchem', 'Keep Off' and with a drawing of a skull and crossbones.

It took at least three hours for the professor to calm down and set about some minor work. But that is what he did. He worked in the Institute until eleven o'clock in the evening, and therefore knew nothing of what was happening outside the cream walls. Both the absurd rumour that had flown through Moscow about snakes of some sort, and the strange yelled telegram in the evening newspaper remained unknown to him, because *Docent* Ivanov had gone to see *Fyodor Ioannovich*[21] at the Arts Theatre, and consequently there was nobody to report the news to the professor.

At around midnight Persikov arrived at Prechistenka and went off to sleep, after additionally reading last thing in bed some English article in the journal *The Zoological Herald*, received from London. He slept, and so did the whole of that Moscow which spun around until late in the night, and it was only the huge, grey block in the courtyard on Tverskaya Street where the rotary presses of *Izvestiya* droned terribly, shaking the whole building, that did not sleep. In the office of the editor an incredible commotion and confusion was under way. Quite frenzied, with red eyes, he was rushing about, not knowing what to do, and sending everyone to the devil. The maker-up followed him around and, with breath smelling of wine, said:

'Well, then, Ivan Vonifatyevich, it's no problem, let them put out a special supplement tomorrow morning. You can't pull the issue out of the press, can you?'

The typesetters did not go their different ways home, but went around in flocks, huddled in groups and read the telegrams which now came in every quarter of an hour the whole night through, becoming ever more monstrous and terrible. Alfred Bronsky's sharp hat was glimpsed in the blinding pink light which flooded the printing-office, and the mechanical fat man creaked and stumped, showing up now here, now there. Doors slammed in the lobby, and reporters kept appearing all night. There were unceasing calls to all twelve printing-office telephones, and the station almost mechanically offered in reply to mysterious callers 'engaged', 'engaged', and at the station the signal horns sang and sang in front of the sleepless young ladies...

The typesetters thronged around the mechanical fat man, and the deep-sea captain told them:

'Aeroplanes will have to be sent with gas.'

'Definitely,' replied the typesetters, 'what on earth is going on, after all.' Then terrible obscene language rolled through the air, and someone's shrill voice cried:

'That Persikov ought to be shot.'

'What's Persikov got to do with it,' came in reply from out of the mass, 'that son of a bitch at the State Farm – that's who to shoot.'

'A guard should have been set,' somebody called out.

'Perhaps it's not even the eggs at all.'

The rotary presses made the whole building shake and hum, and the impression created was that the grey, unsightly block was on fire with an electric blaze.

The day that broke did not stop it. Quite the opposite, it only strengthened it, even if the electricity did go out. Motorcycles rolled one after another into the asphalted yard, alternating with cars. All Moscow rose, and the white sheets of the newspaper dressed it, like birds. The sheets scattered and rustled in everyone's hands, and by eleven o'clock in the morning the newspaper-sellers had insufficient copies, despite the fact that *Izvestiya* was coming out that month in a print-run of one and a half million. Professor Persikov rode out in a bus from Prechistenka and arrived at the Institute. Something new awaited him there. In the vestibule stood wooden crates, neatly edged with metal strips, three in number, dotted all over with foreign stickers in German, and above them reigned one Russian chalk inscription: 'handle with care – eggs'.

Wild joy seized the professor.

'At long last!' he exclaimed. 'Pankrat, break open the crates immediately and carefully, so as not to damage anything. Into my laboratory.'

Pankrat immediately carried out the order, and a quarter of an hour later, in the professor's laboratory, strewn with sawdust and scraps of paper, his voice began to storm.

'What are they doing, mocking me or something?' howled the professor, shaking his fists and turning the eggs in his hands. 'He's some sort of beast, not Byrd. I won't allow people to laugh at me. What are those, Pankrat?'

'Eggs, sir,' replied Pankrat mournfully.

'Hens' eggs, you understand, hens', the devil take them! What the hell do I need them for? Let them be sent to that good-for-nothing on his State Farm!'

Persikov rushed to the telephone in the corner, but did not have time to make a call.

'Vladimir Ipatyich! Vladimir Ipatyich!' thundered the voice of Ivanov in the Institute corridor.

Persikov tore himself away from the telephone, and Pankrat shot aside, clearing the way for the *privat-docent*. The latter ran into the laboratory, contrary to his gentlemanly custom, without removing the grey hat that sat on the back of his head and with a sheet of newspaper in his hands.

'You know what's happened, Vladimir Ipatyich,' he cried

out, and waved in front of Persikov's face a sheet inscribed 'special supplement', in the middle of which a bright, coloured picture stood out boldly.

'No, listen to what they've done,' shouted Persikov in reply, without listening, 'they've taken it into their heads to surprise me with hens' eggs. This Byrd is a proper idiot, look!'

Ivanov went completely crazy. He stared in horror at the opened crates, then at the sheet, then his eyes almost leapt out of his face.

'So that's it,' he began muttering, gasping for breath, 'now I understand... No, Vladimir Ipatyich, just you take a look,' he instantly opened out the sheet and, with trembling fingers, indicated the coloured image to Persikov. In it, like a terrible fire hose, there coiled an olive-coloured snake with yellow blotches in strange, smudged greenery. It had been photographed from above, from a light flying machine, which had cautiously slid over the snake. 'What's that, in your opinion, Vladimir Ipatyich?'

Persikov shifted his spectacles onto his forehead, then moved them to his eyes, peered at the picture and said in extreme surprise:

'What the devil! It's... it's an anaconda, a water boa...'

Ivanov threw off his hat, lowered himself onto a chair and said, banging out every word on the table with his fist:

'Vladimir Ipatyich, that anaconda is from Smolensk Province. It's something monstrous. You understand, that good-for-nothing hatched out snakes instead of chickens and, you must understand, they've laid in the same phenomenal way as the frogs!'

'What's that?' replied Persikov, and his face turned deep red... 'You're joking, Pyotr Stepanovich... Where from?'

Ivanov was struck dumb for a moment, then received the

gift of speech and, jabbing his finger at the open crate, where little white heads flashed in the yellow sawdust, he said:

'That's where from.'

'Wha-at?!' howled Persikov, beginning to cotton on.

Ivanov waved two clenched fists in absolute certainty and shouted:

'Be sure of it. They forwarded your order for snake and ostrich eggs to the State Farm, and the hens' eggs to you by mistake.'

'My God... my God,' repeated Persikov and, turning green in the face, went to sit down on the revolving stool.

Pankrat, completely stupefied by the door, grew pale and dumb. Ivanov leapt up, seized the sheet and, underscoring a line with a sharp fingernail, shouted into the professor's ears:

'Well, now they'll have a jolly story!... What will happen now, I really can't imagine. Vladimir Ipatyich, just you look,' and he yelled out loud, reading the first thing he came upon from the crumpled sheet... 'Snakes are flocking in the direction of Mozhaisk... laying incredible numbers of eggs. Eggs have been spotted in the District of Dukhovo... Crocodiles and ostriches have appeared. Special Forces' units... and detachments of the State Directorate stopped the panic in Vyazma by setting fire to the woods outside the town, which halted the reptiles' movement...'

Persikov, all blotchy, with a bluish pallor and mad eyes, got up from the stool and, gasping for breath, began to shout:

'An anaconda... anaconda... a water boa! My God!' he had never yet been seen in such a state either by Ivanov or Pankrat.

The professor tore off his tie in one movement, snapped the buttons on his shirt, turned a terrible, paralytic shade of crimson and, staggering, with utterly vacant, glassy eyes, he darted off somewhere. A wail flew in all directions beneath the stone vaults of the Institute.

'An anaconda… anaconda…' thundered the echo.

'Catch the professor!' screamed Ivanov to Pankrat, who had begun to dance up and down on the spot in horror. 'Give him some water… he's having a stroke.'

The frenzied electrical night in Moscow was ablaze. All the lights were burning, and there was not a spot in the apartments where lamps with the shades cast off were not shining. Not in a single apartment in Moscow, whose population numbered four million, was a single person asleep, apart from children too young to understand. In the apartments people ate and drank any old how, in the apartments things were shouted out and every minute contorted faces looked out of windows on every floor, directing their gazes into the sky, which was cut to pieces in all directions by searchlights. In the sky white lights were continually flaring up, throwing pale, melting cones back onto Moscow, and disappearing and dying away. The sky was incessantly droning with the very low rumbling of aeroplanes. It was terrible on Tverskaya-Yamskaya Street in particular. Every ten minutes trains arrived at the Alexandrovsky Station[22], assembled any old how out of goods wagons, carriages of various classes and even tank-trucks, thronged by people out of their minds, who ran down Tverskaya-Yamskaya like thick mush, rode in buses, rode on the roofs of trams, crushed one another and fell under wheels. At the station, crackling, alarming gunfire was continually flaring up above the crowd – this was military units stopping the panic of the insane people running along the railway points from Smolensk Province to Moscow. At the station the panes in the windows continually flew out with a frenzied, light sobbing, and all the steam locomotives howled. All the streets were scattered with posters, discarded and trampled, and these same posters gazed from the walls under burning hot crimson reflectors. They were already well known to everyone, and nobody read them. They declared Moscow to be under martial law. They made threats regarding panic and reported that, unit after unit, detachments of the Red Army were already moving to Smolensk Province armed with gases. But the posters could not stop the howling night. In the apartments crockery and flowerpots were dropped and broken, people ran about, catching themselves on corners, undoing and doing up all sorts of bundles and suitcases in the vain hope of getting through to Kalanchevskaya Square, to the Yaroslavsky or Nikolayevsky Stations. Alas, all the stations for the north and east were cordoned off by a very dense line of infantry, and enormous lorries, rocking and jangling with chains, and loaded high with crates, on top of which sat soldiers in sharp-pointed helmets, bristling in all directions with bayonets, carried away reserves of gold coins from the cellars of the People's Commissariat of Finances and enormous crates with the inscription: 'handle with care. Tretyakov Gallery'. Vehicles roared and ran all over Moscow.

Very far away in the sky trembled the reflected light of a fire, and, rocking the dense darkness of August, there could be heard the incessant thuds of cannon.

Just before morning, through an utterly sleepless Moscow that had not extinguished a single light, up Tverskaya, sweeping aside all oncoming traffic, which huddled into doorways and shop-windows, pushing out the glass, there passed, clattering its hooves on the wooden paving-blocks, a snake of many thousands of cavalrymen. The ends of crimson hoods dangled on grey backs, and the points of lances pricked the sky. The crowd, rushing about and howling, seemed to come to life all at once when it saw the columns thrusting forward, cleaving through the slopped broth of

97

madness. The crowd on the pavements began to howl a kind of hopeful invocation.

'Come on the cavalry army!' shouted frenzied female voices.

'Come on!' echoed the men.

'They'll crush!! They're crushing!...' was howled somewhere.

'Help!' came cries from the pavement.

Packets of cigarettes, silver coins, watches flew into the columns from the pavements, women of some sort leapt out onto the roadway and, risking their bones, trudged along at the sides of the cavalry formation, hanging onto stirrups and kissing them. In the unceasing clattering of the hooves from time to time the voices of the platoon commanders soared up:

'Shorten reins.'

There was cheerful and rollicking singing somewhere, and, in the unsteady advertising light, faces in cocked crimson hats looked down from the horses. Continually interrupting the columns of cavalrymen with uncovered faces, strange figures went along, also on horses, wearing strange veils, with breathing tubes over their shoulders and with cylinders on straps behind their backs. Behind them crawled enormous tankers with the longest pipes and hoses, like the ones on fire engines, and heavy tanks on caterpillar tracks that crushed the paving-blocks, tightly closed and with their narrow little sight-holes shining. The columns of cavalrymen were interrupted, and vehicles passed by, tightly sewn up in grey armour, with those same tubes sticking out and with white skulls drawn on the sides with the inscription: 'Gas. Volunchem'.

'Help us, brothers,' they howled from the pavements, 'kill the reptiles... Save Moscow!'

'Mother... mother...' rolled through the ranks. Packets of cigarettes leapt in the illuminated night air, and white teeth were bared at the maddened people from atop the horses. There spilled through the ranks a muffled singing that plucked at one's heart:

> ...*Not ace, nor queen, nor even jack,*
> *We'll smash the reptiles, there's no doubt,*
> *Four on the side – no coming back*[23]...

Hooting peals of 'hurrah' sailed out above all this mush, because the rumour had spread that on a horse in front of the columns, wearing just such a crimson hood as all the horsemen, there rode the cavalry horde's aged and grey commander, who had become a legend ten years before.[24] The crowd howled, and, calming troubled hearts a little, away into the sky flew the booming 'hurrah... hurrah...'

* * *

The Institute was meagrely lit. Events reached into it only as isolated, confused and muffled echoes. Once, under the fiery clock near the Manège, the crash of a volley fanned out; it was looters who had been trying to plunder an apartment on Volkhonka being shot on the spot. There was little vehicular traffic on the road here, it all crowded towards the stations. In the professor's laboratory, where a single lamp burned dimly, throwing a pencil of light out onto the table, Persikov sat with his head on his hands and was silent. Layers of smoke wafted around him. The ray in the box had gone out. In the terrariums the frogs were silent because they were already asleep. The professor was not working and was not reading. To one side, beneath his left elbow, in a narrow column lay the evening edition of telegrams, announcing that the whole of

Smolensk was burning and that the artillery were bombarding the Mozhaisk forest in a grid pattern, smashing the deposits of crocodile eggs laid out in all the damp gullies. It was announced that a squadron of aeroplanes near Vyazma was operating most successfully, having flooded almost the entire district in gas, but that human casualties in these areas were innumerable owing to the fact that the population – instead of leaving the districts in the correct order of evacuation – had panicked, charging about in uncoordinated groups which rushed off at their own peril wherever their noses led. It was announced that in the direction of Mozhaisk a single Caucasian cavalry division had brilliantly won a battle against flocks of ostriches, hacking them all to pieces and destroying enormous numbers of ostrich eggs. In so doing, the division suffered insignificant losses. It was announced by the government that in the event of it proving unsuccessful in containing the reptiles in a zone two hundred kilometres from the capital, Moscow would be evacuated in total order. Office and manual workers were to maintain complete calm. The government would take the severest measures not to permit another Smolensk incident, as a result of which, thanks to the confusion caused by an unexpected attack of rattlesnakes, numbering several thousands when they appeared, the town had caught fire in all the places where burning stoves had been abandoned, and a hopeless, all-embracing exodus had been started. It was announced that Moscow was supplied with provisions for at least six months, and that the commander-in-chief's council was employing urgent measures for supplying apartments with protective armour so as to carry on the fighting with the reptiles on the very streets of the capital, in the event of the Red Armies and aeroplanes and squadrons not succeeding in containing the invasion of the reptiles.

The professor read none of this, he looked ahead with glassy eyes and smoked. Apart from him there were only two people in the Institute – Pankrat and the housekeeper, Marya Stepanovna, continually in floods of tears and sleepless now for the third night, which she was spending in the laboratory of the professor, who did not wish to abandon his single remaining extinguished box for anything. Now Marya Stepanovna was ensconced on the oilskin couch in the shadow in the corner, and was in silent doleful thought, watching the kettle of tea intended for the professor starting to boil on the tripod of a gas burner. The Institute was silent, and everything happened abruptly.

Hateful, ringing cries were suddenly heard from the pavement, so that Marya Stepanovna leapt up and shrieked. In the street the lights of lanterns began to be glimpsed, and Pankrat's voice responded in the vestibule. The professor took this noise badly. He raised his head for a moment, muttered, 'Just listen to them raging… what can I do now…' And fell once again into torpor. But it was disturbed. The Institute's forged doors leading out to Herzen Street began to rattle terribly, and all the walls began to shake. Next the continuous layer of plate glass in the neighbouring laboratory broke. Glass rang and fell out in the professor's laboratory, and a grey cobblestone bounced through the window, knocking down the glass table. The frogs jumped in the terrariums and raised a cry. Marya Stepanovna began running about and screaming, she rushed to the professor and seized him by the hands, shouting: 'Run away, Vladimir Ipatyich, run away.' The latter rose from his revolving chair, straightened up and, folding his finger into a little hook – whereupon his eyes acquired for a moment their former sharp brilliance, reminiscent of the former, inspired Persikov – replied.

'I'm not going anywhere,' he pronounced, 'this is simply stupid – they're running around like madmen... Well, and if the whole of Moscow has gone mad, then where on earth will I go? And please stop shouting. What am *I* to do with anything? Pankrat!' he called, and pressed a button.

He probably wanted Pankrat to put an end to all the fuss, which he never liked in general. But Pankrat could no longer do anything. The din ended with the doors of the Institute opening, and the tiny cracks of gunshots were carried from afar, and then the entire stone-built Institute started to rumble with running, cries, the breaking of glass. Marya Stepanovna grabbed hold of Persikov by the sleeve and started dragging him somewhere; he beat her off, drew himself up to his full height and, as he was, in a white coat, went out into the corridor.

'Well?' he asked. The doors flew open, and the first thing that appeared in the doorway was a soldier's back with a crimson chevron and a star on his left sleeve. He was retreating backwards from the door, into which a furious crowd was pressing, and he was firing a revolver. Then he started running past Persikov, shouting to him:

'Professor, save yourself, I can't do any more.'

His words were answered by Marya Stepanovna's scream. The soldier slipped past Persikov, who stood like a white statue, and disappeared in the darkness of the winding corridors at the opposite end. People were flying out of the doors, howling:

'Smash him! Kill...'

'The enemy of the world!'

'You let the reptiles loose!'

Contorted faces, ripped clothes began to jump in the corridors, and somebody fired a shot. Sticks could be glimpsed. Persikov retreated a little, half closed the door that led into the laboratory where Marya Stepanovna kneeled in horror on the floor, spread his arms, like a man crucified... he did not want to let the crowd in, and shouted in irritation:

'This is plain madness... you're absolutely wild animals. What do you want?' He began to howl: 'Get out of here!' and ended the phrase with the abrupt cry familiar to all: 'Pankrat, see them off.'

But Pankrat could no longer expel anybody. With a broken head, trampled and torn to shreds, Pankrat lay motionless in the vestibule, and ever new crowds tore past him, paying no attention to the firing of the police from the street.

A short man on simian, bowed legs, wearing a ripped jacket and a ripped, skew-whiff dicky, outstripped the others, tore up to Persikov and with a terrible blow of a stick split his head open. Persikov rocked, began to fall onto his side, and his last words were:

'Pankrat... Pankrat...'

Marya Stepanovna, who was guilty of nothing, was killed and ripped to pieces in the laboratory, the chamber where the ray had gone out was broken up into tiny bits, they broke the terrariums up into tiny bits, slaughtering and trampling the maddened frogs, they smashed the glass tables to pieces, they smashed the reflectors to pieces, and an hour later the Institute was ablaze, corpses lay around beside it, cordoned off by a column of men armed with electric revolvers, and fire engines, pumping water from taps, were pouring jets into every window, from which, buzzing, long flames were breaking out.

CHAPTER TWELVE
A Frosty Deus in Machina[25]

On the night of the 19th to the 20th of August 1928 an unheard-of frost struck, one such as none of the long-time inhabitants had ever before seen. It came and stayed for two days, reaching minus eighteen degrees. Maddened Moscow locked all the windows, all the doors. Only towards the end of the third day did the population realise that the frost had saved the capital and those boundless expanses it owned, on which the terrible calamity of 1928 had fallen. The cavalry army outside Mozhaisk, which had lost three quarters of its strength, had begun to suffer from exhaustion, and the gas squadrons could not stop the movement of the vile reptiles, coming in the direction of Moscow in a semicircle from the west, south-west and south.

They were suppressed by the frost. The loathsome flocks could not endure two days at minus eighteen degrees, and in the last ten days of August, when the frost had gone, leaving only dampness and wetness, leaving moisture in the air, leaving the greenery on the trees damaged by the unexpected cold, there was nothing left to fight. The calamity was over. The woods, fields, the boundless marshes were still piled high with multi-coloured eggs, sometimes covered with the strange pattern – unprecedented, not from these parts – which Faight, who had disappeared without trace, had taken for muck; but these eggs were utterly harmless. They were dead, the foetuses inside them had been finished off.

Boundless expanses of earth still rotted for a long time as a result of the innumerable corpses of crocodiles and snakes, summoned to life by the mysterious ray, born on Herzen Street in the eyes of a genius, but they were no longer dangerous, the delicate creatures of putrid, hot, tropical swamps died in two days, leaving over the area of three provinces a terrible stench, decay and purulence.

There were long epidemics, for a long time there were mass diseases caused by the reptile and human corpses, and for a long time yet the army was about, no longer supplied with gas though, but with sappers' equipment, kerosene tanks and hoses, cleansing the earth. It completed the cleansing, and everything had ended by the spring of 1929.

And in the spring of 1929 Moscow again began to dance, to burn and to spin with lights, and again, as before, the traffic of mechanical conveyances shuffled, and above the dome of the Church of Christ there hung, as if on a string, the sickle moon, and on the site of the two-storey Institute which burnt down in August 1928, a new Zoological Palace was built, and it was headed by *Privat-docent* Ivanov. But Persikov was no more. No more did there arise before people's eyes the contorted, convincing hook, formed from a finger, and nobody heard any more the squeaking, croaking voice. The whole world talked and wrote for a long time yet about the ray and the catastrophe of 1928, but then the name of Professor Vladimir Ipatyevich Persikov was cloaked in mist and died away, as died away too the red ray itself, discovered by him on an April night. It did not prove possible to get this ray again, although sometimes that elegant gentleman and nowadays permanent Professor Pyotr Stepanovich Ivanov did try. The first chamber was destroyed by the frenzied crowd on the night of Persikov's murder. Three chambers were burnt at the Nikolskoye 'Red Ray' State Farm in the first battle of squadron with reptiles, and it did not prove possible to restore them. However simple the combination of lenses and mirrored pencils of light might have been, it was not put together a second time, despite the efforts of Ivanov. Evidently something special had been required for this, besides knowledge, something which only one man in the world had possessed – the late Professor Vladimir Ipatyevich Persikov.

NOTES

1. A.V. Lunacharsky (1875–1933).

2. The name of a restaurant, a beer bar and a variety revue club in Moscow at the time.

3. H.G. Wells's novel of 1904, in which a race of intellectually developed giants is bred by the use of special food, only then to be victimised.

4. SPD (in Russian, GPU or *Gosudarstvennoye Politicheskoye Upravleniye*) was a secret police forerunner of the KGB formed in 1922.

5. Excuse me, Mr Professor, for the disturbance. I work on the Berlin *Tagesblatt*.

6. I'm very busy at the present moment and I cannot see you at all.

7. K.V. Radek (1885–1939), a member of the Central Committee of the Communist Party.

8. Between ourselves.

9. The Lubyanka was the popular name for the secret police headquarters on Moscow's Lubyanskaya Square.

10. G. I. Rossolimo (1860–1928) was a neuropathologist at Moscow University.

11. The name was doubtless suggested by Portugal's national emblem being a cockerel.

12. A department store alongside the Bolshoi Theatre.

13. The innovative director V. E. Meyerhold (1874–1940) did use trapezes in staging Russian classics, but only suggested in a lecture the use of semi-clothed actors in Alexander Pushkin's history play as part of a new approach to tragedy. The other names and titles in this passage are largely a similar blend of invention and distortion by Bulgakov.

14. Edmond Rostand (1868–1918) and his play *Chantecler* (1910).

15. An invented abbreviation adapted from that of an actual organisation also referred to in the text, Volunchem – The Voluntary Society for Cooperation in Building the Chemical Industry, established in May 1924.

16. A reference to Charles Evans Hughes (1862–1948), US Secretary of State 1921–5.

17. In Russian, *Tsekuba*: the Central Commission for the Improvement of the Life of Academics, formed in 1919 and based on Prechistenka from 1922.

18. Tchaikovsky's opera of 1890 based on the story by Alexander Pushkin.

19. Tchaikovsky's opera of 1879 based on Pushkin's novel in verse.

20. *The Russian Word* was a daily newspaper founded in 1895 and published from 1897 by Ivan Sytin (1851–1934).

21. The historical tragedy *Tsar Fyodor Ioannovich* (1868) by Alexei Konstantinovich Tolstoy (1817–75).

22. Now the Byelorussky Station, Moscow's main terminus for trains from the west.

23. The song is a parody of the Communist anthem, the *Internationale*.

24. An allusion to the leader of the Red Cavalry during the Civil War, S. M. Budyonny (1883–1973).

25. God in a Machine. Bulgakov's chapter title includes this inexact rendering in Russian of the Latin term *deus ex machina*, literally 'god from a machine', referring to the device in Classical Greek drama of bringing a god onto stage by mechanical means to resolve an apparently insoluble moment of crisis.

Mikhail Bulgakov was born in Kiev in 1891. In 1909 he entered medical school, where he began writing; his early stories were based on his medical experiences, and resulted in his *Notes of a Young Doctor*. In 1913 he married Tatyana Lappa, and she proved a considerable support when he was later to suffer from a morphine addiction. He worked as a doctor in Kiev in the years 1918 and 1919, where he witnessed first the German occupation, and then the invasion of the Red Army. Soon after this he gave up medicine in favour of pursuing a writing career; he had, by this time, written numerous short stories and a number of plays for local theatres.

In 1921 he moved to Russia, where he worked for a number of different publications, including the newspaper *Gudok*. His first collection of short stories, *Diaboliad*, was published in 1925; that same year he wrote *Heart of a Dog*, only to see it confiscated by the police. He was by now facing increasing pressure from his communist critics and, in 1928, he was refused permission to travel abroad. It was forbidden for his plays to be performed, although this did not prevent Bulgakov from continuing writing; in 1928 he had begun what was to be his masterpiece, *The Master and Margarita*.

In mid-1929 he began petitioning Stalin for permission to leave Russia. Stalin refused, but allowed Bulgakov's play *The Day of the Turbins* to be staged. The conflict between the artist and the State from then on became the key theme in Bulgakov's writing. He continued working on *The Master and Margarita* until his death in 1940, and although it was published some years after his death, the full, uncensored, version did not appear until 1989.

Hugh Aplin studied Russian at the University of East Anglia and Voronezh State University, and worked at the Universities of Leeds and St Andrews before taking up his post as Head of Russian at Westminster School, London. His previous translations include Anton Chekhov's *The Story of a Nobody*, Nikolai Gogol's *The Squabble*, Fyodor Dostoevsky's *Poor People*, Leo Tolstoy's *Hadji Murat* and Ivan Turgenev's *Faust*, all published by Hesperus Press.

SELECTED TITLES FROM HESPERUS PRESS

Author	Title	Foreword writer
Pietro Aretino	*The School of Whoredom*	Paul Bailey
Jane Austen	*Love and Friendship*	Fay Weldon
Honoré de Balzac	*Colonel Chabert*	A.N. Wilson
Charles Baudelaire	*On Wine and Hashish*	Margaret Drabble
Giovanni Boccaccio	*Life of Dante*	A.N. Wilson
Charlotte Brontë	*The Green Dwarf*	Libby Purves
Giacomo Casanova	*The Duel*	Tim Parks
Miguel de Cervantes	*The Dialogue of the Dogs*	
Anton Chekhov	*The Story of a Nobody*	Louis de Bernières
Wilkie Collins	*Who Killed Zebedee?*	Martin Jarvis
Arthur Conan Doyle	*The Tragedy of the Korosko*	Tony Robinson
William Congreve	*Incognita*	Peter Ackroyd
Joseph Conrad	*Heart of Darkness*	A.N. Wilson
Gabriele D'Annunzio	*The Book of the Virgins*	Tim Parks
Dante Alighieri	*New Life*	Louis de Bernières
Daniel Defoe	*The King of Pirates*	Peter Ackroyd
Marquis de Sade	*Incest*	Janet Street-Porter
Charles Dickens	*The Haunted House*	Peter Ackroyd
Fyodor Dostoevsky	*Poor People*	Charlotte Hobson
Joseph von Eichendorff	*Life of a Good-for-nothing*	
George Eliot	*Amos Barton*	Matthew Sweet
F. Scott Fitzgerald	*The Rich Boy*	John Updike
Gustave Flaubert	*Memoirs of a Madman*	Germaine Greer
Ugo Foscolo	*Last Letters of Jacopo Ortis*	Valerio Massimo Manfredi
Elizabeth Gaskell	*Lois the Witch*	Jenny Uglow
Théophile Gautier	*The Jinx*	Gilbert Adair
André Gide	*Theseus*	

Nikolai Gogol	*The Squabble*	Patrick McCabe
Thomas Hardy	*Fellow-Townsmen*	Emma Tennant
Nathaniel Hawthorne	*Rappaccini's Daughter*	Simon Schama
E.T.A. Hoffmann	*Mademoiselle de Scudéri*	Gilbert Adair
Victor Hugo	*The Last Day of a Condemned Man*	Libby Purves
Joris-Karl Huysmans	*With the Flow*	Simon Callow
Henry James	*In the Cage*	Libby Purves
Franz Kafka	*Metamorphosis*	Martin Jarvis
Heinrich von Kleist	*The Marquise of O–*	Andrew Miller
D.H. Lawrence	*The Fox*	Doris Lessing
Leonardo da Vinci	*Prophecies*	Eraldo Affinati
Giacomo Leopardi	*Thoughts*	Edoardo Albinati
Nikolai Leskov	*Lady Macbeth of Mtsensk*	Gilbert Adair
Niccolò Machiavelli	*Life of Castruccio Castracani*	Richard Overy
Katherine Mansfield	*In a German Pension*	Linda Grant
Guy de Maupassant	*Butterball*	Germaine Greer
Herman Melville	*The Enchanted Isles*	Margaret Drabble
Francis Petrarch	*My Secret Book*	Germaine Greer
Luigi Pirandello	*Loveless Love*	
Edgar Allan Poe	*Eureka*	Sir Patrick Moore
Alexander Pope	*Scriblerus*	Peter Ackroyd
Alexander Pushkin	*Dubrovsky*	Patrick Neate
François Rabelais	*Gargantua*	Paul Bailey
François Rabelais	*Pantagruel*	Paul Bailey
Friedrich von Schiller	*The Ghost-seer*	Martin Jarvis
Percy Bysshe Shelley	*Zastrozzi*	Germaine Greer
Stendhal	*Memoirs of an Egotist*	Doris Lessing
Robert Louis Stevenson	*Dr Jekyll and Mr Hyde*	Helen Dunmore
Theodor Storm	*The Lake of the Bees*	Alan Sillitoe